£11 99

THE QUEEN'S CORSAIR

No-one in the small Devonshire farming community expected delicate Mary
Newman to live to maturity, let alone
to marry. She surprised them when she
eloped with a young mariner, who carried
her off to London. Mary settled down to
married life, believing that the romance of
her elopement would be all the excitement
she would ever know and that her future
would be one of contented domesticity. But
her husband's name was Francis Drake,
and her future was to be different from
anything she could have imagined.

THE QUEEN'S CORSAIR

by
Judith Saxton

Dales Large Print Books
Long Preston, North Yorkshire,
England.

British Library Cataloguing in Publication Data.

Saxton, Judith
    The Queen's corsair.

A catalogue record for this book is
available from the British Library

    ISBN 1-85389-886-4 pbk

First published in Great Britain by Robert Hale & Co.,
Ltd., 1976

Copyright © 1976 by Judy Turner

Cover illustration © Franklin by arrangement with Allied
Artists

The moral right of the author has been asserted

Published in Large Print 1999 by arrangement with
Judy Turner

Dales Large Print is an imprint of
Library Magna Books Ltd.
Printed and bound in Great Britain by
T.J. International Ltd., Cornwall, PL28 8RW.

Author's Note

Mary Newman is not mentioned in historical records, save for her marriage to Drake and her death; therefore I have had to rely heavily upon my imagination to construct Mary's story. However, the framework of her life is that of her husband's comings and goings, and in this respect at least, there is evidence in plenty.

Dedication

For Ted Dutton and Vic Simons,
of Prestatyn Writers' Circle,
who started it all!

1

FARM LIFE

The kitchen of the Newman farm was warm enough; and on this cold January day with the snow covering the cobbled yard and icicles as long as your arm hanging from the byres, it was not too bad a place to be. So thought Mary, as she laboured with her elder sister, Annie, to cut the tough, salted pork into shreds.

Elsewhere in the house they could hear their mother chivvying the two little serving wenches, whilst their younger sisters, Ruth and Kate, could be seen through the kitchen window as they scurried across the yard from the cow byre to the dairy. Mary caught Annie's eye and they exchanged smiles. Pleasant to be in the kitchen preparing a meal, without the sound of their mother's sharp tongue rattling on and on as she clattered across the dirty rushes in her working pattens. Too often for their liking, she found jobs for her elder daughters to do in the draughty old farm buildings so that they had to throw worn cloaks over their working gowns, pull their white caps further down over their ears, and chop cattle fodder or mix pigswill with their chilblained, puffy hands.

It was not too bad for Annie, a big, cheerful girl with rosy cheeks and well-covered limbs. But even though she was fifteen, Mary still looked a child. Small, thin and pale, with a tendency to chesty coughs, people often shook their heads over Mary. When she was a tiny, serious toddler, 'You'll not rear that one,' they had said grimly. But now she was of marriageable age, folk said, 'She'll not marry, for what farmer would want a sickly, ailing wife who can help with neither the sowing nor the harvest? Who can scarcely heave the cooking pots from the fire, unaided?'

Her sisters were good to her, trying to keep the harder work for themselves, and see that skinny Mary got the lighter tasks. It was not easy, for their mother thought that each of them should do her share, and was quick with a scolding or a beating for a daughter who seemed not to take her turn at every task.

'Do you ever wish you were a fine lady, Annie?' Mary's voice, as she felt the salt from the pork sting her cracked and roughened hands was wistful.

'Aye, indeed I do. But when I marry, I'll have little maids to run my errands for me. I'll wield a stick across their shoulders if they don't come a-running with more wood for the fire, and I'll see 'tis *they* who cross the farmyard to chop turnips.'

Annie laughed boisterously and Mary smiled too. Annie was too kind for such goings-on she knew. Her sister was going to be married in the summer, to a grand sturdy lad from a farm near Tamar. He had fallen in love with Annie's placid disposition and her creamy skin, and was going to carry her off to his father's farm, on the easy hills overlooking the river, until he could afford to build a little house on the land his father had promised him. Annie would be all right, her handsome William would see to that.

'I'll miss you when summer comes,' Mary said a trifle dolefully. 'Imagine, up on Dartmoor on a day in high summer, with Sheepstor above us, purple with heather, against a sky bluer 'n a blackbird's egg. Us girls a-picking and a-pulling at the lichen to sell down at Plymouth market; and no Annie to make us laugh and ease the work.'

'You'll be fine wi'out me, you'll see,' Annie told her optimistically. 'You've got sister Ruth to lend a hand until you or she wed, and that'll not be for a while yet, and Kate always works with a will when the weather warms, especially up on the moor, with the wind fresh on her cheek, and her head full of Dartymoor haunts.'

'You're right, of course. And anyway, 'tis selfish not to rejoice in your happiness,' Mary agreed. 'Bless me, we'd best hurry with this pork—a pox on the toughness of it—or mother will be here fit to burst into flames at our laziness.'

Both girls worked with a will and very soon the pork was shredded onto the plates and quantities of steaming cabbage added from the pot which had been boiling on the fire. Annie, red faced from exertion, doled out a mess of dried peas cooked to a pudding, and Mary darted round putting out loaves of coarse brown bread, and jugs of their own home-brewed ale.

When the preparations were complete, Annie went to the kitchen door and called out that the meal was ready, then to the big back door leading into the yard. As she swung it open the cold air scrambled into the room so that steam, which had been invisible, could suddenly be seen, rising

11

in puffs from the cabbage, spurting from Annie's lustily opened mouth as she called the men.

''Tis only a simple meal,' Mrs Newman said as she pulled her petticoats round her and lowered her tall, raw-boned frame carefully onto the wooden bench. Her small, sharp eyes darted round the table searching for some fault, failed to find it, and returned to gaze challengingly at her husband. 'A simple meal,' she repeated, 'but us had fine fare in plenty at Yuletide, and today we'm cleaning the house and too busy for much cooking.' Her husband sat down without replying and began shovelling the food into his mouth without more ado but Mary's brother, Richard, winked at his sister as she toyed with the unappetising plateful.

'Ah, our bellies were well-lined over the Christmas season,' he asserted stoutly. 'And even this ... this simple food is better than poor Harry is probably getting, eh Mary?'

Mary shivered and nodded. She thought that at least their food was plentiful and untainted, which one could not say with certainty, of Harry's provender. For Harry, her favourite brother, had taken ship with John Hawkins on one of his adventurous voyages to seek his fortune, and this winter of 1569 had been sharp throughout so that they could well imagine what agonies of cold and hardship poor Harry might be suffering.

'The lad may be in a better land,' Mrs Newman said complacently. She took a long pull of ale and wiped her mouth on her sleeve. 'After all, they left Plymouth a year ago last October; that means they've been gone near on fifteen months. Rumour has it that Hawkins is dead, killed by those cursed Spaniards. Our Harry might 'a died early on in the voyage for we'm not folks of importance and no messages would be sent back to us. The first we'll know of our lad is when the ships anchor with him aboard or not, as God wills.'

Mary felt the colour draining from her face. Harry! The beloved brother, the one who had escaped from the toil and hardships of the farm to the greater toil and hardships of a life at sea; but who might well make their fortunes for them. The Newman farm was sizeable, but not big enough to warrant a living for both the Newman lads and their father, with his insatiable thirst and foolish bad management. Master Newman was popular neither with his labourers nor his neighbours. He was known to be a hard man who would not help willingly with another's harvest until his own was safe in his barns, and then he had to be reminded that work was owed. Little was thought of the way he treated his children, for many believed that youngsters learned best with a stick across their shoulders, but when the drink was on him, Farmer Newman was dangerous to man and beast. With the additional suspicion that all the Newman sheep had not been born of

Newman stock, there was reason enough for the faintly veiled dislike with which the farming community regarded Master Newman. Yet despite his father, Harry had always been popular, and the neighbours always remembered to ask after him when they met one of his brothers or sisters at work in the fields or down in the town of Plymouth.

Mary put a spoonful of cabbage into her mouth and ate it without thinking. Harry was such a wonderful brother. So full of jokes and merry talk. He loved Mary more perhaps because she was small and frail, and was always buying her little gifts. He had promised to bring her many wondrous things when he came back from his voyaging—and now their mother sat there shovelling pork into her mouth, her legs clamped as firmly to the floor as though she were rooted, and carelessly announced he might well be dead!

Mary said obstinately, 'I'm sure Harry isn't dead. I'm *sure.*'

Mrs Newman stopped pushing food into her mouth for a moment to stare at her daughter, eyes bulging with disbelief. Mary so rarely gave an opinion and when she did so, it was apt to be spoken in an apologetic tone. Now here she was, pink cheeked at her own daring, flatly contradicting her mother!

Mrs Newman was opening her mouth to tell Mary a thing or two, when she heard a muffled sound from the yard outside. Someone—or something—was crossing the snow, they could hear the squeak of the thick white blanket being compressed under a foot, and the soft hushing as whatever it was approached the long drift down the centre of the yard and pushed through it. Something loomed dark against the low lattice, and Mrs Newman gave a shriek.

'"Tis the phantom hunter!' she said, and a cacophony of sound broke out with the little girls screaming, Richard laughing, and Farmer Newman saying gruffly, 'Phantom nothing, woman! What phantom would

16

enter our yard in broad day and come reeling across the window light like a bedazzled barn owl? 'Tis some snow-led traveller.'

As he finished speaking the back door burst open and a figure lurched into the room, accompanied by a sudden flurry of snow and an evil little wind which nipped at the skin, bringing gooseflesh up on the girls' faces and causing Master Newman to roar, 'Shut that door, whosoever you be!'

The cloaked figure shook snow off his broad-brimmed hat and said in an unmistakable Devon accent, 'Hold hard, another du follow,' and sure enough another man came wearily through the doorway and swung the door closed behind him.

''Tis Jack and cousin Sam, come a day early,' squeaked the youngest girl, Kate, and Mrs Newman, accepting the guess, said with an attempt at good humour, 'Well, well, and you've caught us with a poor thin dinner on our table, boys. But us ate so rich over Christmastide ...'

A muffled laugh came from the taller of the two men and Mrs Newman looked uncertainly at them, then to the lurchers lying before the fire waiting for the scraps from the table. The biggest, Taff, got to his feet with widening eyes, whilst a snarl came slowly from between his big, white fangs. But little Tossy, the stout and elderly retriever whose dark eyes were milky with age, suddenly bared her teeth in an ecstatic grin whilst her tail described arcs of excitement and pleasure.

'Her knows me,' announced the tall man, then pulling his hat from his head cast it down on the floor, revealing fully for the first time his heavily bearded and weatherbeaten countenance. 'Don't 'ee know me, mother?' he said plaintively, but with twinkling eye.

Before Mrs Newman had a chance to speak, Mary, with a shriek of delight, was across the room and casting herself upon her brother's chest. Heedless of the joint stool which she had knocked flying, and or the mired and drenched garments he was wearing, she clung to him, saying 'Harry, my own Harry! Oh, I've missed you, I have. I just knew you weren't dead, though. I knew it.'

'Come now, little maid, don't cry,' said Harry gruffly, stroking Mary's shaking shoulders. 'Dead? Me? I should say not. More thanks to my friend than aught else, mind. Hey now Mary, I've not introduced my friend. Let go of I now, or he'll think us strange, unwelcoming folk. Frank, this is my family, and this is Frank Drake, who captained the *Judith* which was my ship and who saved my life a hundred times if once.'

Mary emerged from her brother's embrace and smiled shyly at the stranger, then at her mother's hasty command ran to the fire to spread the men's cloaks out to dry before its warmth. She spared the strange Captain Drake no more than a cursory glance, having eyes only for Harry's broad and substantial figure which a moment ago had been no more than a vague, well-loved memory. She heard her mother putting on her 'company' voice, saying that the girls would get the men a decent dinner and her son Richard would lend them dry clothing, and then Harry's friend spoke for the first time.

'Our first task, Mistress Newman, should be to wash, for we have the salt and grime of many days on our skins. But the pump in the yard is frozen solid.'

'I'll heat water and take it to Harry's room,' Annie said quickly. 'Richard, you take the men upstairs whilst us girls get on with the work.'

With the departure of the men, the kitchen became a hive of activity once more. Ruth, only a year younger than Mary but because of her more mature figure usually taken for the elder, fetched linen towels and some of the best soap and Mary helped Kate to prepare the plump capon which had been intended for the cousins' delectation the following day. Even Master Newman was kept busy, though he grumbled beneath his breath, mulling a jug of home-made plum wine with a red hot poker.

Annie, coming down the stairs after having delivered jugs of hot water, said to Mary, 'A captain, Mary! And him no older than our Harry, or I'm much mistaken. To think of him befriending our brother!'

Mary, peeling turnips, said merrily, 'No one is too good for our Harry, Annie. He seems a pleasant young man, though nowhere near as tall and handsome as our brother.'

'I think him very handsome,' Ruth chipped in somewhat defiantly, and Mary thought with an inward groan, oh no, is Ruth in love *again?* Ruth was notoriously susceptible and though only fourteen had been in and out of love a dozen times in the past couple of years.

Annie cast a shrewd eye over Ruth's carefully bent head, and said casually,

'Why, how could we tell whether the stranger is handsome or not, Mary? Both he and our Harry be well grimed, snowed on, and travel-stained. They look a pair of ruffians, if the truth be told.'

'Aye, a couple of drowned rats,' agreed Mary, laughing. 'Now come on Ruth, do! If you moon over the young man's looks our mother will be laying into us in front of Harry and his friend for being so slow. She'll ruin Harry's homecoming by doing that, for he's the gentlest lad.'

Yet it seemed that either Mistress Newman was fonder of her eldest son than she appeared, or the presence of a captain at her dinner table made her careful of her manners. When the two young men came downstairs, faces shining from a hearty application of soap and water, both clad in clean clothes a trifle too small for them, Mrs Newman was all smiles.

'We've prepared a good, hot meal for you,' she said, ushering them to the table, 'and when you've eaten and drunk your fill perhaps you might tell us of your voyage, for I've no doubt you've many a tale to tell, if you'm willing.'

Mary smiled to herself at her mother's hopeful tone, and the mingling of her broad Devonshire accident with what Mary had dubbed the 'company voice'. But nevertheless, she drew nearer to the table, determined not to miss a word of Harry's story, though her mother might scold.

At last the capon was plump no longer, the vegetable dishes were empty, the wine had sunk low in the jug. As Harry reached out a brown hand for the dish of nuts he looked hopefully at his friend. 'Can you tell 'em the tale, Frankie?' he enquired. 'I'm no hand at story telling and you know better than I what occurred.'

'Very well, Harry. Mistresses, I will gladly sing for such an excellent supper by telling you of our adventures, if such they could be called.' He leaned back in his chair and Mary noticed that in the light from the tallow candle his hair gleamed redly, like a well polished chestnut.

'We traded along the Guinea coast at first—or tried to,' he began. 'But the Portuguese refused to trade unless they were compelled.' He grinned. 'So sometimes we captured, and Captain Hawkins paid later, and sometimes we fought and took by right of conquest. We had some adventures that you'll scarcely believe! Our ships being too big to trade close inshore, we sent men up-river in small boats, and one of them got capsized when a hippopotamus rose up from a mudbath and swamped her. The men swam for one of the other boats and got there safely, for hippopotamus are mild enough creatures. River horses, the natives call 'em. But the rivers have plenty of crocodile too, and *they* don't chew grass! We got some negroes, mainly by capturing the boats they were loaded in and paying later, with barter goods which we had in our holds. Then in a place called Sierra Leone, our luck changed. We had been wondering whether to go on to the Gold Coast, to try to buy gold dust, but we had a hundred and fifty slaves and it seemed a doubtful enterprise. Then this local chieftain approached Master Hawkins and announced that his tribe was going to declare war on another, a native township of eight thousand souls, called Conga. Well, I'll spare you the more grisly details of the battle and just tell you that we won and the chieftain gave us many slaves from the Conga tribe. Grateful enough they were, too, for those of their brethren who did not come with us were most foully butchered by their enemy.'

'How did they foully butcher them?' asked Kate, with all the ghoulish interest natural to a nine-year old. Frank Drake chuckled, leaning back in his chair and eyeing her with smiling indulgence. 'Little maid, they ate them,' he said frankly. 'Cannibals, many of the natives on that part of the coast. Is that awful enough for you?'

'Dreadful!' said Kate, shudderingly. 'Did they roast them?'

'Hush, you dreaful child,' Mary said, laughing, but Mrs Newman gave her youngest daughter a sharp clout across the ear, which made Kate sink into resentful silence.

'After we had sailed,' resumed Drake, smiling encouragingly at little Kate, 'we made our way to the port of Borburata in the province of Venezuela. Our Captain Hawkins had been there before it seemed, and knew that good trade could be had, if it were allowed. And we did do well there, despite the Governor, Ponce de Leon, telling us that he could not allow us to trade. He had to say that I suppose, since Philip of Spain has forbidden his provinces to trade with the English, but he did not take action against us. In fact, we cleaned and careened all the vessels during our stay on those pleasant and hospitable shores.'

'And we learned a few words of Spanish, did we not, Frankie?' interposed Harry, tossing his friend a walnut kernel and aiming the shell at the fire. 'For when you are trading it is as well to speak some of the language at any rate.'

'We learned a few phrases,' admitted Drake with a grin. 'But before we had done much more than that, we sailed again and this time called at Rio de la Hacha, an ill-omened place to be sure for two years earlier, with Lovell's fleet, we experienced a taste of Spanish treachery there.'

'But *we* experienced no treachery—not at Rio de la Hacha,' protested Harry, lazily lounging in his chair and enjoying the story as much as anyone.

Drake grunted. 'Not this time,' he admitted grudgingly, 'But curse it, Harry, you must admit they made us pay for their precious trade concessions. We had to take the town and burn a few houses, and then we had to dig up the treasure which they had concealed before they would trade.'

'It was that pig of a Governor, Castellanos,' Harry reminded his friend. 'The

27

Spanish settlers could not have been more eager to trade. Anyway, we did well from the place, eh, Frankie?'

'Well enough,' agreed Drake. 'But better at our next port of call—Santa Marta. My, but that was a mad business! We were requested to pretend to take the town by force, the Governor there being as sensible and down to earth as Castellanos was foolish and flown by pride and lies. So we arranged which derelict house should be blasted to smithereens by our cannon, dressed our men in armour and had a merry day of pretend battle, in which no one was hurt nor any property damaged, except for the derelict house I mentioned before. After that, the Governor staged a scene before witnesses, begging us not to burn the town which would leave them at the mercy of the natives and the climate, and Hawkins solemnly promised to hurt no one nor any property if he was granted the right to trade. We had a merry time there, did we not, Harry? Dancing, banquets, friendly faces on all sides. I'll wager our knowledge of the Spanish tongue came on apace in Santa Marta.'

'Aye, you're right. And we had the best of victuallings,' Harry said reflectively. 'Not that anything could make up for what came after, mind.'

'No. Nothing. Well anyway, from Santa Marta we sailed to Cartagena, having in truth little left to trade but some fifty negroes. However, the Governor there refused to have anything to do with us and would not even let us water our ships, which right should not be denied to any Christian company save perhaps in time of war. So our Captain Hawkins said no matter, we could run straight for England and home now without any further stops and should indeed do so, for the season of hurricanes would soon be approaching. But we met severe weather earlier than is usual in those parts and one of our fleet, the old *Jesus of Lubeck*, could not stand such conditions and had to run before the wind.

We followed her of course. Why, she was the treasure house for all our gains, being the biggest, most majestic ship in the fleet, though also the least seaworthy. So we stuck close to her, and when the wind had blown itself out we were in shoal water, too shallow and dangerous to try to repair the damage done to the *Jesus,* for she carries a deep draught. Our only course seemed to be to run for San Juan de Ulua, which we accordingly did. The officials there were awaiting the plate fleet, which brings all the silver and gold of the Indies to fill the coffers of Philip of Spain.' He laughed shortly, without amusement. 'They took us for the fleet, in fact, our royal standards being so faded and weatherbeaten that they could not see the device until they were alongside us. Our Captain explained that we were innocent merchants, and had no designs on the *flota,* and it was eventually agreed that we might anchor and mend the *Jesus* so that she could last out until we reached an English port.

But once again, ill-luck favoured us. The plate fleet made good time, and arrived outside the harbour before we had really had time to begin work on the *Jesus*. However, we had command of an island where the Spaniards had their guns, and we manned the guns and decided to let the fleet into the harbour.'

'I'd have kept 'em out,' growled Harry, staring into the depths of his wine glass. 'I didn't see then why our admiral agreed to the treacherous swine entering the harbour and I don't see it yet.'

'Harry, how could Hawkins deny entry to the plate fleet, when in the first place it was a Spanish fleet trying to enter a Spanish harbour, in the second place when he had announced we were peaceful merchants, and in the third place when to leave them at anchor outside that poor harbour would have meant their inevitable wrecking as soon as the wind changed its quarter?' demanded Drake hotly. 'God, man, he did what he had to do, neither more nor less. But in the event, a Spaniard is a Spaniard and there's no changing him. We exchanged hostages, and fair words. Yet within five days of the entry of the fleet the expected treachery happened, for whilst the Spaniards were still denying any thought of an attack, one of the hostages at meat with Captain Hawkins, drew out a dagger and tried to stab him. After that, I suppose everyone saw only their own fight, so to speak. We were taken pretty much by surprise, never realising quite how complete the treachery was until we saw soldiers brought from inland pouring over the sides of the harbour whilst guns blazed from their so-called merchantmen and we answered them with everything we'd got—though a large number of our men were ashore at a banquet supposedly given in their honour by the sailors from the *flota*. We speedily saw what the result of such carnage must be, for we were very much out-numbered. Earlier, we on the *Judith* had grumbled a little, for we anchored very near the harbour mouth where we felt all the turbulence of the ocean whilst yet at anchor. Yet it was the saving of our lives. We warped out of danger—for there was little our small guns could do—and waited for Captain Hawkins to reappear with the ships which could sail. We could see that two ships at least—the *Jesus* and the *Minion*—were ready with sails set to leave the harbour. Indeed, we had men from the *Jesus* already on board, for she was listing heavily and Hawkins was beginning to take the contents out of her to a place of greater safety than any the old ship could provide. What then happened we could not tell, save that the *Minion* sailed out alone, heavily laden with men, and lay about a quarter of a mile outside the harbour. We waited for them to join us, but they did not attempt to do so and heavily laden as we were, I thought it best to let Hawkins sail the Minion out to us rather than that both vessels should run the risk of the lee shore close to which he lay.'

'And when did he join you?' asked Richard, now too involved with the tale to remember his customary shyness.

'He did not,' Drake said shortly. 'We heard the wind coming up, and voices, and were fearful that if we delayed longer in the darkness the Spaniards might creep up to us in the night and board us when we were defenceless. Indeed, such was our armoury that had they attempted to attack in broad daylight we could have done little. So we sailed out into the ocean and when daylight came, we scanned the horizon for the *Minion,* but not a corner of her sail, not the tip of her mast, was to be seen. So we came slowly homeward, and although we must hope and pray that some of our men survived, I fear it will only be to live a life of slavery and oppression in Spain.'

'So out of the fleet that set sail from Plymouth, only the *Judith* got back?' Mary's voice was small and forlorn.

The young man turned and smiled at her rather sadly. 'Yes, I'm afraid so. I went at once to William Hawkins' house and told him the news, then rode to London—for the Queen shared in the venture, the *Jesus* was her ship—and though everyone is vowing vengeance on Spain it will not bring back our great Admiral.'

'What reprisals will be taken?' asked Richard, letting his curiosity get the better of him once more.

'As to that, the Queen heard rumours that the venture was a disaster, so she put an embargo on money which Philip of Spain had borrowed from the Italian, Spinola. It was to pay his troops with I believe, or some such thing, but our Queen realised that once it was in his hands she would get no return from the loss of the money put into the voyage. It is said that when he heard, Philip got in such a passion that he slapped an embargo on English property in the Netherlands, which was where the money would have gone. Elizabeth, not to be outdone, then put an embargo on Spanish property in England which is a lot at the moment. That is a fair start, for vengeance is hardest when it hits Philip's pocket.'

'The money would have been on those fleets which were attacked by French pirates in the channel, and took refuge in our ports, some of them in Plymouth,' remarked Mary thoughtfully. 'Here we are near enough to Plymouth, yet in these conditions,' she gestured to the snow which was falling again, 'we hear less of what goes on there than they do in London.'

'Yes, and no doubt Harry and I ought to be in Plymouth,' said Drake, with a smile. 'But for tonight at any rate, we shall be grateful for your hospitality.'

'And tomorrow you shall know it in full measure, and eat of the best the house can provide,' Master Newman said heartily, and Mary wondered with a small stab of fear how soon the drink in him would twist his present good humour into a reasonless fury. But Harry and Drake were weary, and he ushered them up to the main bedchamber, insisting yet again that they should honour his home by spending a few days with them.

Before their voices had faded out of hearing, Mary was on her knees picking up bits from between the rushes, and lamenting that they could not now lay new ones. However, she cleared half the floor and began to scrub the tiles whilst Annie trod lightfoot over all, setting the breakfast dishes ready. 'Do you like Master Drake, Mary?' Annie said, as her sister threw the worst of the rushes on to the fire and sat back on her heels to watch them burn.

Mary considered, her head on one side so that the weight of her hair in the net she wore swung heavily against one shoulder. 'He's a proper gentleman,' she said at last. 'But has it occurred to you Annie, that there is something odd about him coming here? Something odd, too, in the way he and Harry glance at each other, almost uneasily? I like what I know of him, which isn't much, and I'd like to know what the pair of them are up to.'

Yet when she knew, together with the rest of England, she still did not know the mystery behind the young captain who slept beneath their roof.

2

CHANGE OF CIRCUMSTANCE

'What is our brother up to now, insisting that he and his handsome friend must go into Plymouth in this weather?' Ruth's voice was sharp and aggrieved as she joined Mary in the warmth of the cowshed.

Mary, her head buried in the cow's warm flank as she hissed milk into the wooden pail with an expert hand, said, 'They had a message from the town, Ruth. I hear 'twas good news, for Master Hawkins and many of the other men are back, though in a sorry state. Captain Drake has gone into the town to find out exactly what happened and I expect Harry felt he should accompany his friend.'

Ruth sniffed. She had enjoyed the

company of a young man about the house who was neither a brother nor a farm labourer. She had dressed with care, brushing her hair with a will, slapping her cheeks vigorously to make the fine red colour show up the blue of her eyes, whitening her nose with a little pinch of flour from the bin, and making her sisters tighten her stays for her until the poor garment creaked and groaned and protested. She had not failed to notice, either, that Frankie Drake had eyed her with friendliness. Now she pouted, and moved further into the shed to escape from the nipping cold in the yard.

'I don't suppose we shall see *him* again,' she said crossly. 'Glad enough of our hospitality he was, when he thought his friend dead; now he'll stay in a fine house in Plymouth and be treated like a hero, no doubt.'

Mary thought not. She had spoken to Harry before they left the farmhouse, and Harry had been worried. ''Tis like this,

Mary me wench,' he had said hurriedly. 'The messenger says the Hawkins family are outraged with Drake for sailing straight home in the *Judith,* instead of lingering to see whether he could help the rest of the fleet. If he is going to be in trouble, I'd as lief be with him.'

But she told Ruth none of this. Some inner caution urged her to say nothing. She merely replied in rather a bored voice, 'No, we'll see nothing more of the captain.' She finished her task and the two girls went into the house, each carrying a pail of foaming milk.

The days passed, and life in the farmhouse went on much as usual. With the extreme hardness of the weather they could not take stuff to the market, not that they had much to spare. They lived off the farm and off the food which was always stored in anticipation of a bad winter, though like most of the country they rarely ate fresh meat after Christmas, except for a few wild geese shot down as they flew, honking sadly, overhead.

Mary wondered how her favourite brother and his friend fared in Plymouth; whether they were really in disgrace—in prison, even. Then, as suddenly as they had come and gone, Harry and Drake reappeared. They came, two small figures against the elements, battling against another snowstorm. Mary was in the cowshed and went across to open the backdoor for the travellers, then slipped inside with them. For once, the usually busy room was deserted and though the smell of the rushes was none too sweet, the air at least was warm to frozen hands and feet.

Hanging the men's sodden cloaks over a stool in front of the fire, Mary asked anxiously, 'Did all go well?' and tried to tell herself that she asked only for the sake of her tall, mischievous brother; that the stranger's welfare worried her not at all.

The men exchanged glances. 'We can trust our Mary, Frankie,' Harry said at last. 'But not a word of this to anyone, wench.

Just at the moment, our Frankie's none too popular in Plymouth. Captain Hawkins put the tale around that we in the *Judith* deserted him, forcing him to abandon men to a terrible fate with the Spaniards because the only other ship which survived from the fleet that entered San Juan, the *Minion,* could not have reached England so heavily burdened.'

Mary grasped Harry's hand urgently. 'Surely they know that isn't true?' she cried. 'You had no means of knowing they would ever escape from that ...' she hesitated over the little-known word, '... that carnage.'

But Frank Drake was shaking his head. 'I know now I should have waited, mistress. At the time it seemed the sensible course, to run for home and England before we, too, were blasted out of the the sea by some Spanish traitor. But I should have waited, even though we risked capture; and in any event, capture was by no means certain. The *Judith* is fleet and far more manoeuvrable than any Spanish vessel.' He gave an exclamation of rage, smacking his fist into his palm. 'If only I had thought, instead of taking it for granted that there was nothing more I could do! Why John Hawkins landed one hundred men on the coast of Mexico; had there been another vessel standing by we could have taken some of them at least. And of the men who sailed in the *Minion* forty-five died on the voyage. Why, for the last seven days before they sighted land they gnawed on an ox-hide for they had no food left. Believe me, my good friend—my only friend—John Hawkins has every reason to reproach me. There will never be another chance for me with his ships after this and I cannot blame him.'

'I see,' said Mary forlornly. 'But Harry is your friend, sir; and I—I am very much your friend, as are my sisters. What will you do now?'

'We shall rest for a day or so, then make our way to Gravesend or Tilbury and join the Queen's navy,' Harry said bitterly. 'Frankie here is determined to earn command of another vessel, and that is one way, if the Hawkins' patronage is to be withdrawn. I am with him, of course,'

'So it will be yet another short stay with us?' said Mary with an attempt at nonchalance. 'Well, you'd best go up to your room and send down those clothes for drying. You can put them outside the door and I'll pick them up when I bring you some hot water to wash in.' She eyed the bags they carried. 'You've fresh garments in there?'

'Yes, all we need for a journey across the country,' said Harry. 'We'll share your supper and spend the night in my chamber, then we'll have a good breakfast to cheer us and be off on this new venture.' Mary could hear the bitterness in her brother's voice, and knew what a disappointment it must have been to him to share in his friend's disgrace. But she knew her Harry; he would stand by his friend.

The next morning she awoke early, determined that the two travellers should fare well before setting off into the world of snow and ice that surrounded them but as soon as she entered the kitchen she knew their guests would not be leaving for a while. Thick and soft, the snow had piled up as high as the windows so that the kitchen was drowned in a green snow dusk, even first thing in the morning. It was impossible for any one to leave the farmhouse except to make their slow way across the yard to the beasts in the byre.

And by the time the thaw came, Drake had a good reason for not leaving the Newman's farm. During the dimmery days enclosed by the weather into enforced idleness, he had not wasted his time. He had fallen deeply in love with a delicate face of childish pallor, with smooth, nut-brown hair which felt like softest silk to his calloused hands. With slender fifteen year old Mary, whose parents had despaired of ever seeing her attract a lover. And Mary was in love with him.

★ ★ ★ ★

'Your sister Ruth eyes us strangely,' Drake remarked. 'Yet I'm sure she must know my intentions towards you are honourable.'

Mary was silent. She could have told him Ruth was jealous, that she resented a less attractive sister making a love match with the man she believed to be a successful sea captain. But it would only have harmed Ruth, and anyway as yet, Frank Drake had not spoken openly of a desire to make her his wife. Instead, she said hopefully, 'Shall we go up on the moors, Frank? In the sheltered spots at this time of year, primroses bloom, and soon we'll be able to pick the hardy daffadowndillies, when the March wind sets them dancing.'

'Are your tasks over for the day, little maid?' Drake asked diffidently. He knew that farmers' children worked hard; indeed since he had taken ship aboard a bark when he was ten he had seldom known a holiday;

but he knew his own strength, both physical and spiritual. He bent every task, no matter how unpleasant, to his will so that he learned something of use from it and thus continually widened his knowledge and abilities. But he had never seen a young girl driven as Mary was driven, day in, day out by her parents. Now that the weather was more clement she worked in the fields, sowing by hand, rooting out the sturdy weeds that fought to strangle the young wheat, walking behind the two big shire horses, pushing the clumsy wooden plough with all her frail strength. She toiled over the beasts, feeding, grooming, and mucking out their quarters and worked like a serving maid in the house also, knowing no rest until late at night, when the girls finally redded the kitchen and went wearily to their pallet beds.

But somehow, with Frank's help, Mary had finished her tasks with the whole sweet spring afternoon before her, and she had no intention of being found idle and given work to do in the house. 'Come on, Frankie,' she urged. 'Once we're over the brook and amongst the rocks no one will bother to search for us.' She glanced at him wickedly under her lashes. 'Witches can't bind you with a spell once you've crossed running water,' she teased and Frank had to grin because 'witch' was one of the kinder things he had called her mother in his mind.

'We'll take her back a bunch of primroses,' Mary planned busily. 'And as for Ruth, she likes you well enough; I shouldn't worry over her.'

They crossed the brook and began to climb onto the wild and heathery slopes and then as Mary had foretold, they began to see the shy spring flowers half hidden by rough, tussocky grass, in every sheltered hollow.

The soft sunlight painted even the grim old standing stones with gold, and Mary enlivened the walk with a good few bloodcurdling stories of the many and various haunts of the moor. 'Phantom huntsmen with great slavering phantom dogs,' she said with relish. 'We call them the wish hounds. If you come across them and follow after, they'll lead you to your death. And plenty of phantom monks of course, since Henry VIII did away with the abbeys. But we've worse haunts than that, to my way of thinking, in the standing stones. Some say they are innocent maidens, turned to stone by witchcraft. They have the power to move, certainly. I've seen them myself, when Annie and I have been caught by mist. Then it is that they take a walk to stretch their cramped legs, poor souls. And there are the will o' the wisps, which lead travellers into the bogs. Not only travellers, animals too. 'Gone to Dartymoor stables' we say in these parts, when an animal is lost without trace, for the bog is bottomless, you know.'

'What about the sheep that have gone to Newman's stables?' said Frank with a chuckle, but Mary, though she laughed with him, looked apprehensive.

''Tisn't safe to joke about it,' she said solemnly. 'Harry used to tell my father that one day the wickedness of his sheep-stealing ways would catch up on him. But there, our sheep are more plentiful this year, and have lambed well. Maybe the Dartmoor lambs are safe from *that* hazard, at least.'

In a small, straggling wood beside a stream they found some catkins, and Mary pointed out a coffin stone to Drake, where bearers of the dead had laid their burden on a conveniently slab-shaped rock whilst they had a rest, and some had idly chipped crosses out of the rough granite surface.

'I wouldn't like to be here at night,' she said thoughtfully. 'I love Dartmoor, Frank, yet it can be frightening. Sometimes when I'm up on Sheepstor I can feel the presence of something great, grim, and terrifying. Yet commonsense says it is only the boulders, and the whistle of the wind.'

'What was it you were telling me about a royal favourite haunting a pool up on the moor?' said Frank teasingly. 'Nothing much great, grim and terrifying about *him*, from all accounts.'

Mary laughed. 'You mean Piers Gaveston, the young man favoured by Edward II? Ah well, he tempted the fates by going to Crazywell pool and asking the spirit of the waters to tell him what his fate would be. He didn't want to believe it, of course; he always thought the King would take him back into favour. So now they say he haunts Crazywell, luring unsuspecting travellers to their death in the water, or to hear their own death sentence pronounced.'

'Do you believe all these tales, Mary?' Drake asked, picking his way through a number of small boulders.

'Not in bright sunshine,' acknowledged Mary gaily. 'But believe me, Frank, if you've ever been lost on the moor, or caught in one of the blinding rainstorms, or tricked by its mists, you don't just believe, you *know* it is all true and you are sure you will be the next victim. Oh look, a sheep with twins!'

'I see her. What is unusual about that?'

'She'll not rear them both,' Mary said wisely. 'It's all right though, they are our lambs. But I'll take the smaller of the two home where it can be bottle fed.' She lifted the tiny creature up and held it securely in her own thin arms.

Frank looked at her, with the hair falling down over her shoulder and her face softened with affection for the lamb and before he had thought twice, he had taken her in his arms and kissed her soundly.

Mary neither blushed nor scolded. She smiled sweetly and said 'I *have* enjoyed our afternoon together, Frank. But we had better be getting home now or my mother will be annoyed with us.'

They walked into the kitchen as the early dusk of March was falling, to find the family assembled and about to have their evening meal. Frank braced himself for questions, disapproval, downright annoyance even. But instead, Mrs Newman rushed forward, scolding Mary fondly for dirtying her gown. Drake was astonished, but not more so than Mary. Her gown, an old one, had once been of blue fustian but age and constant wear had faded it to a dirty grey, and it was hard to see how Mary could have been accused of dirtying a garment so incredibly thin and worn. Then Drake realised that not only the family were present. Standing before the fire, legs apart, hands behind his back, was a sturdy old gentleman in his best visiting clothes. His doublet and hose were wine coloured velvet and the gown which almost reached his ankles was also of velvet, black, worked in red and white and gold round the sleeves and neck.

Drake raised his brows. Who was this then, who had come a-visiting as soon as the thaw set in? He glanced at Mary, but she was blushing a deep pink, gazing down at her gown as though its state alone were responsible for her heightened colour.

Seeing the young man at a loss, Mrs Newman said affably, 'This is Captain Drake, Master Poynter. Master Poynter has a prosperous farm on the hills overlooking Tamar, Frank. He has come looking for a willing maid to help his wife run the farmhouse; one well-versed in the ways of dairy and stillroom. I told her there's none had so good a hand with butter as our Ruth, but it seems he misremembered her. 'Twas Mary who caught his eye last hiring fair, and 'tis Mary he's come to fetch.'

'He wants Mary? But how will you manage without her, when Harry and I are off to sea once more? Who will make the pies—game pies, saffron pies, warden pies—none have a lighter hand with pastry than mistress Mary.' Drake was grasping at straws and he knew it.

'Why, surely we'll have a struggle to make the work get done; 'twill be worse in the summer when Annie leaves us for her husband. But Mary will be getting good money, Master Drake, which will enable us to buy the grain we lack, and to replenish our beasts at market when the young stock goes under the hammer. Besides ...' she glanced at him slyly out of the corner of small acquisitive eyes '... Master Poynter has three great sons who work his land with him. 'Twas one of them 'membered our Mary as a tasty little lass who was gentle and biddable. Master Poynter says he'll see no harm comes to her during her two years hire, and at the end of it, she'll wed wi' Dick Poynter and be a lady with a farm of her own. If so be she does her work right, and pleases all,' she nodded righteously.

Drake could say nothing. He cursed himself for not giving voice to his intentions earlier, but he had been so sure of Mary! Her mother continually bewailed the girl's pallor, her lack of spirit and her foolish speechlessness when in the company of young men; Drake had been sure he would be accepted eagerly as Mary's suitor. But he had not wanted to be able to offer his love nothing but a doubtful reputation and a dingy lodging in Plymouth. He wanted to give her security, a life free from toil, and enough money to be able to indulge in small luxuries such as nice clothing, and perhaps a little maid to help her in the house. He had dreamed of going on a voyage and laying the proceeds in Mary's lap, so that her parents would also realise what a good husband Mary was getting. And now? It looked as though the good husband would be Dick Poynter, if indeed the fellow bothered to marry her. Drake looked at Mary's slender figure and thought she would not have much strength to fight off any advances the man chose to make, once she was living in his mother's house as her paid servant.

Mary waited a moment, making herself look as small and useless as possible, glad of her worn, shabby gown and the mud-clogged pattens on her feet. But the face of Master Poynter, round and red as a dutch cheese, continued to beam down at her, and in the end, she put the little lamb down near the fire and went upstairs in silence to change into her best things as her mother had bidden her, with Ruth clattering importantly beside her.

All through the evening, the two young people hoped and prayed for a chance to escape; to talk over what was happening to them. Harry, watching, knew his parents too well. They would not give Mary's hand in marriage to Frankie now. The chance of allying themselves with a family as important as the Poynters could not be lost. His best-loved sister would go the strange farmhouse and if she managed to keep her virtue from the Poynter lads for two years (he remembered them well; spoken of as more lustful than lusty), then she would wed Dick Poynter and live a life of comparative ease. If not? He shook his head, frowning to himself. Without a dowry and lacking even her maidenhead to offer a suitor, he doubted if she would ever free herself from the shackles of a hired wench. Then the visitor got to his feet, and Mrs Newman fetched Mary's cloak and threw it round her shoulders.

'She shall go with you now, as you wished, Master Poynter,' she said cheerfully. ''Tis not far from home, Mary, so when your new mistress gives you leave, you might come home to see how we fare. We shall expect her wages quarterly, as agreed.' She handed Mary a small bag and said kindly enough, 'Your clothes, daughter. Only a few things mind, since Mrs Poynter has said she'll provide your working dresses and a good supply of caps, aprons and petticoats. But I've packed your best stammel kersey kirtle, with the hair coloured gown and the embroidered shift you have made yourself for Annie's wedding, since they're all too small and narrow-made to fit any of your sisters.'

Frank imagined her in the red and tan of her best clothes, offset by her own large blue-grey eyes and white skin, and had to grip his hands into fists until he could feel his nails biting into the flesh. At that moment Mary's small milky body was more desirable to him than the fastest ship in Her Majesty's navy, and he would have thrown his future prospects overboard to be able to say 'she is mine.'

But already Master Poynter was leading Mary towards the door. 'Come, little maid,' he said heartily, 'my son has driven over with the horse and cart to fetch us, so we'll arrive at your new home in style. Kiss your sisters and your parents and we'll be on our way.'

Before the bewildered girl had done more than turn mutely towards her mother, she was soundly kissed by that person and ushered firmly out of the door. The last Drake saw of his love was her small, wistful face framed by the shining brown hair as she looked back over her shoulder towards the lighted kitchen doorway; then she was pushed, not unkindly, into the cart.

As the rattle of the wheels and the clatter of hooves faded into silence, Harry said abruptly, 'Frankie, I'm for bed. We've a deal of talking to do, we mustn't be held up for women's matters. Mother, I must tell you I think you've dealt very badly with my sister; God knows you've girls a-plenty to do your work for you and I blame myself for going away and leaving you with only Richard to help with the farm work. But Mary has worked as hard as any son, sowing and reaping on the land. What need was there to sell the girl away to those Poynters? I'll wager the maid will be forced to lie with each of the lads in turn until she quickens with child, for they'll want a fruitful wife for their son. And if she doesn't please them, what will they do, think you? She'll be driven back here with her reputation gone, and you'll hire her out to another and another, until she falls dead from fatigue. She's a good worker but she's not strong as you well know.'

'If she's brought back here unwed, the Poynters will pay me a good sum, for I've Master Poynter's written word to say so,' said Farmer Newman truculently. 'But 'tis my belief that young Dick is really hot for her, and will wait out the two years. Think, boy; he remembered the wench from hiring fair last September, and she isn't a rosy, blooming piece like my other daughters, but a pale, skinny little creature. I've not done so badly by the girl.'

Harry gave him a baffled glare, then took the stairs two at a time, with Drake close on his heels.

'Tomorrow, I shall shake the dust of this place from my feet,' Harry said fiercely. 'Why, 'tis close on April and we have to make our way to a port.' He looked sideways at Drake and then said awkwardly, 'You had a fancy for my sister, did you not, Frankie? A pity you hadn't pledged yourselves before my parents. They would have welcomed such a marriage I am sure and would have found it impossible to send Mary away. But since things have turned out this way, we should linger here no longer. We cannot help Mary; her fate for two years is to toil in the Poynters' farmhouse and if all goes well, at least she'll be wife to a man of substance.'

'I shan't forget her,' Drake said broodingly. 'I'll write to her, Harry. She shall not forget me, either. If it is humanly possible, I shall make my claim on her before the two years is up.'

'My poor Frank, what makes you think Mary could read your letters? I assure you she could not! She can neither read nor write. As for making a claim on her, I doubt if you could do so. She is in bondage for two years, so far as I can see. Now come, let us get some sleep so that we can be on our way first thing in the morning.'

3

THE POYNTERS

'The work at Poynters is hard, yet nothing like so hard as 'tis at home.' Mary sat by Annie's side in the parlour, enjoying the warmth of the bright May sun which came streaming through the open window.

Annie looked up from sewing her trousseau. 'Are you happy, lass?' she asked curiously. She wondered how the younger girl managed all by herself up at the big house.

'Happy? Well, happy enough,' conceded Mary. 'There are three hired wenches, we do the housework and help with the cooking and such; dairy and stillroom work, mainly. 'Tis lighter by far than the work our mother laid on my shoulders.

But ... oh, I can't explain, Annie. Partly it is being a hired wench which goes against the grain, and partly the way young Dick Poynter looks at me. Shrewdly adding me up against all the well dowered farmers' daughters he meets at market. I think sometimes, he almost hates me for attracting him.' Her eyes widened with surprise. 'Annie, as though I would *want* to make him love me!'

'Do you not, then, Mary? Surely it were better that he should love you and marry you when the two years is up than you be returned home, unwed?'

'I suppose so,' said Mary with a sigh. She stretched and yawned, catlike, in her chair. 'Our mother's first words were "Have they paid you yet?" and not a murmur as to my happiness or well-being.'

'You don't still hanker after that young mariner, who went off with Harry, Mary?'

'He was in love with me, Annie, and I with him. He would have married me, and no nonsense about working for his mother for two years, either. But we weren't promised.' She sighed, remembering the afternoon in the spring when they had wandered round the foot of the tors, so lighthearted and sure of one another's affection. It seemed years ago, and not only a couple of months, for the countryside was no longer bleak, leaves clustered thick and shiny on the trees and the blossom was white on plum and pear.

'You look much fatter and prettier, Mary,' Annie told her sister. 'Happen it is the food and such, and the lighter work. But you've more colour to your cheeks and more shape to your figure.'

'Happen it is,' said Mary with a laugh. 'Happen I shall be sixteen come September, Annie. It was high time my shape began to show itself. And the decent clothes do help. I've a good friend in the sewing woman. She does little else but sew for the people on the big farms, and when she comes round to help Mistress Poynter she usually makes me a little bit of a cap, or brings some ribbons to brighten a gown. She altered my corsets—so big and clumsy, the ones our mother had given me, they almost burst out of my gown—and recut my bodices, letting in some pieces when my breasts began to swell.'

'Why is she so kind to you?' said Annie, plying her needle vigorously. 'I wish I had more skill with my needle—you should ask her to give me lessons.'

'I think at first she wished to gain my favour so that she might sew my brideclothes,' said Mary, with a wise little nod. 'But since then, she has been kind because I probably seem friendless and alone in that big house.'

'Why should that be so?' asked Annie, ever practical. 'You've two other hired wenches who do the same work as you and doubtless others besides. You surely have friends a-plenty.'

Mary did not argue because she did not wish to distress her sister, but as she walked back to Poynters across the lonely stretches of moor, with the scent of the gorse in her nostrils and the sound of the bees gathering honey all around her, she thought how far from happy was her lot. Because Mistress Poynter had gone to considerable lengths to show the other hired wenches that Mistress Mary Newman was no ordinary young woman but the desired bride of her eldest son, the girls, Meg and Sally, had shown Mary coldness in public and real spite and dislike when they got her to themselves. They saw to it that as far as possible Mary got the hardest jobs, the place farthest from the fire and—when they realised she disliked it—tried to push her into Dick Poynter's path.

Mrs Poynter herself was a small, brisk woman, by no means unkind, who would have liked to see her eldest son wed without any to-do and certainly had no desire for her future daughter-in-law to work as a paid servant in her house.

But as Mary soon realised Mrs Poynter had little or no say in the running of the household. Farmer Poynter was a man who knew his own mind and it was not greatly to his liking that his son should marry into a family like the Newmans, with a drink-sodden father and a scold for a mother, to say nothing of doubtful dealings amongst other people's herds. So he had made the condition—that the young woman should live in the house for two years and work for his wife—half hoping that his son's infatuation would die, with the girl so near, or at any rate that she might prove herself capable of child bearing before Dick rushed into marriage.

And though Dick had not made more than token advances of friendship towards her, Mary had little hope that this state of affairs would continue. She had been with the family less than two months, yet already Dick was quick to come to her side whenever the work permitted, and had persuaded his mother and presumably his father, since that gentleman had made no objection, that it was right and proper for Mary to sit with them in the parlour of an evening, helping Mrs Poynter with the work of embroidering bedcurtains with a biblical scene.

Mary appreciated the fact that whilst embroidering in the parlour, she could neither be larking in the kitchen with menservants who might have tried to take advantage, nor be pressed into tasks like candlemaking and rendering fat down for soap, which made one's hair and clothing smell for days. But on the other hand, her fellow servants (for what else was she?) began to dislike her more, because she was one of them yet privileged beyond them.

So she sat meekly plying her needle full of red, or scarlet or golden coloured silk, at her task of embroidering the burning bush. Mrs Poynter did not trust her young charge with the figure of a wild-eyed and astonished Moses, who beside

70

being considerably overcome by the sight of Mary's burning bush, had begun his existence with very few clothes on; this lack she was remedying, however, by the addition of a rather stiff looking doublet and a pair of skin tight hose. Mary, condemned to the flames, she thought humorously, was often sadly bored. At home, when the sisters worked at their stitchery in the evenings though she might be bone weary and aching in every limb, yet her tongue had worked overtime, jesting and laughing with Annie, Ruth and Kate. But here, scarcely a word was uttered. She and Mrs Poynter stitched, Farmer Poynter snored, and Dick Poynter stared. Mary, wriggling resentfully, thought he spent every evening mentally stripping her down to her shift or less. Still, she realised that as yet he had done little else and she should be grateful for that, at least.

She sometimes wondered why Mrs Poynter never remarked on the absence of her other two sons, Amos and Luke, from the family evenings. She knew that the younger, Luke, usually spent his time larking with the maids in the servants quarters, and that Amos spent long hours on the accounts when he was not visiting his own bride to be, at her home some miles distant. In the end she came to realise, grudgingly at first, that the Poynters were very undemanding parents. They expected their sons to work hard all day but they did not try to influence the way in which the boys spent their leisure.

Although Mary did not precisely enjoy the embroidery sessions, at least they were a haven of peace in her unquiet life amongst the other servants, and they were also short; Farmer Poynter had no intention of wasting the good wax candles his wife insisted that they burn in the parlour, leaving the tallow ones for the servants. So before Mary had completed more than one tongue of flame, and whilst Mrs Poynter stitched a few more hairs onto Moses' ever-lengthening beard, the master of the house would heave himself out of his chair to bid the servants go up to their rooms and douse their lights, and Mary would scuttle off upstairs to the attic she shared with five other women, and strip down to her shift. Then she would curl up on her hard little pallet and sleep soundly enough.

For in sleep, came her greatest satisfaction. Often enough, yet never often enough for Mary, she would dream of Frankie Drake. Sometimes in her dream he would come for her, and take her away to his ship; sometimes she would run from the Poynter farm into the summer dream-sunshine—and run on and on, over boundless moors, until she found Frankie. Once, to her horror, she floated above the sea on gull's wings and saw below her on the great expanse of endless ocean, a small ship where she knew her love lay dying. She tried to reach him, but they chased her off as the gull-shape she was, and to her distress they buried him in the vast, dreaming sleep of the sea. At other times they danced round a maypole which suddenly became a ship's mast, and the captain of the ship was always Frank, or a mysterious dream-peddlar would come selling ribbons, and turn into her Frank at the touch of a hand.

Yet when she did see Drake again, the meeting could scarcely have been less like her dreams.

★ ★ ★ ★

By the time summer was truly upon them, Mary was able to assure Annie that she really was happy at the Poynter farm. She had grown very fond of the kindly mistress of the house, who loved her sons so much that she was willing to teach Mary any trick of fancy cooking or sewing which would one day make her a better wife for Dick. And Dick himself had a far stronger and nobler personality than Mary had guessed as he sat and stared at her across his mother's parlour. He had opportunities of being alone with her, but when he achieved this, he liked to talk to her of what sort of home she would like, whether she thought it better to make sufficient butter and cheese for the market, or whether one should make enough for one's own use, and save the grazing of additional beasts. He told her too, of his abiding love of the land he had known since he was a baby. The Poynters had farmed this land time out of mind, he said proudly. He took her wandering over Dartmoor, telling her tales and legends, making her laugh and weep, but always when she left him she was unwillingly impressed by what she had learned.

'Dick Poynter is not a man to be taken lightly,' she said to Meg. The other girl laughed and pinched Mary's cheek. They had become good friends once the servants realised that Mary did not mean to take advantage of her position, and felt the awkwardness of it even more keenly than they did.

'Thee've taken thee time to discover 'un,' she remarked. 'Us couldn't make out why thee wasn't rubbing thy hands at such good fortune as being wed one day to our Dickon.'

'Yes, well. I had dreams of my own, you know. They didn't include Poynters farm at all,' Mary said defensively.

'Canst dream of Dickon now, maid?'

Mary reddened uncomfortably. It seemed so dreadful to know and acknowledge that Dick was an honourable and good man, that his love was to be treasured. Yet to know that she did not long for him as she longed for a chance-met mariner who had kissed her once; to acknowledge to herself that she would marry Dick, bear his children, comfort him in sickness and work with him to better their land and their lot. But love him? After all, what did she know of love! Perhaps she would learn what love really meant, in Dick's arms.

Out loud, she said, 'Why should I dream

of Dick, Meg, when he is here, within reach?'

Meg eyed her out of surprisingly shrewd eyes, brown as blobs of fresh toffee. 'If thee loves, thee'll dream, wheresoever he be,' she stated dryly.

'I can't remember what I dream,' Mary said flippantly. 'Once I dreamed I was a seagull. Then I expect I loved another seagull. It was a marvellous feeling, being able to fly, gliding on great, outstretched wings over the sea which was so far below that the waves looked like ripples on a bright blue pond.'

Meg laughed indulgently. 'Thee can't help but dream of our Dickon one day,' she said confidently. 'He'm best lad thee are ever like to meet, wench.' She scrutinised Mary's face, then said easily, 'Why, thee've nigh on two years left to learn of him. Thee have to love Dickon, for he loves thee so well.'

The remark left Mary speechless, but it did nothing for her peace of mind.

She began watching Dick and noticed that many of the farmers' daughters who came to the house with their parents, many young girls who came up from Plymouth to buy fresh butter, or cream for a special occasion, would have been glad of Dick's glances. But he spared them none. He had eyes for no one but Mary. She began to feel a terrible sense of guilt. Who was she, after all, to fail to be pleased by this personable and kindhearted young man? The servant girl, child of a drunken farmer and nagging mother who had sold her into servitude for the sake of a few pounds a year. She should be grateful that Dick even looked on her with kindness; she should pour her love out unstintingly at his feet for the happiness she had found under his roof if for no better reason. Yet she could not do it.

For Dick, I am as dry as the standing stones, and as empty of feeling, she realised with wonder. But for Frankie, I am a bubbling well of love and warmth, which wants to spill out so that I could cry my love aloud to the stars, if they would listen.

For the first time in her life, her emotions troubled her. She wept into her pillow because Frankie had forsaken her, and she wept because she was a generous girl and knew that however much she might give to Dick, she could not give him what he wanted. Her body and her wifely duties were hers to dispose of where she would, and Dick should have all the outward signs of her affection. But she could not give what had been granted elsewhere, and she did not understand her own lack. She began to lose the glow of contentment which had blessed her when she first lived at the Poynters' farm. She became edgy and moody, trying to avoid Dick yet anxious not to give offence to one so tender hearted.

In the end, she cornered Meg one day in the dairy, when they were churning butter, and decided to tell the older girl as much as she could.

'So you see, Meg, it isn't that I don't love Dick, so much as that I've given some sort of love to Frankie, and I cannot get it back for the asking,' she explained miserably. 'I know you're right, and Dick is a good man. I know I am very fortunate to have gained his affection. But I can give him nothing! You were wrong when you said one day I'd dream of Dick; I didn't understand what you meant at the time but I do now. Dick can have all the ordinary things, and gladly, but I cannot give him my dreams for whether I will or no, they belong to Frankie, even if he cares not a jot for them or me.'

Meg stopped her work to listen. Then she turned her eyes, grave for once, on Mary, and spoke. 'Thou art in a fine old tangle,' she said soberly. 'But thou art young, little maid. Time may still the ache of longing which beats for your mariner and in its place you may find contentment in Dick's company. When time has passed, his memory must grow dim, but Dick is here, and his goodness will fill thy heart. Thou will yearn no more to swing on the wind as a seagull, but will be content to toil happily with thy children at thy knee.'

'But what of Dick?' Mary whispered. 'What of him, Meg? Is he not to expect more from me than wifely obedience and a child each year?'

'When a man loves as Dickon loves thee, is it not enough?'

With that, Mary had to be content and as June sped on and July approached, with her sister's wedding day to be anticipated with pleasure, her own affairs sank to the back of her mind. Not to be forgotten, but to lie at least for a while at any rate, so that she might enjoy being an attendant to the bride, and enjoy the feast and the dancing afterwards. It became a sort of anodyne for the ache of Frankie's absence to tell herself that she would worry about her own troubles after the wedding. Until then she would enjoy her work about the house and her comradely relationship with Meg. After the wedding, she promised her conscience, I will take myself in hand and look facts in the face. But until then, let me be fifteen, and carefree! Let me shelve the responsibilities of growing up!

4

THE WEDDING

'Mistress Mary, we'm going to the market. Tomorrow your sister Annie weds wi' the eldest Garret lad, and we're all bidden to join in the merrymaking. You would ha' gone anyway of course, seeing as how you're the bridal attendant but would you not like to come into Plymouth wi' us, to buy your sister some pretty gew-gaw for her bride-day? You can take some money out of your quarter's wages, surely? They'm due today.'

Mary looked consideringly at Mrs Poynter, and that lady had the grace to blush. 'My mother will think ill of me if I take home to her wages which be so much as a groat short,' she pointed out.

'Aye, perhaps. But I've given 'e a little extra, see, for all the work you've put in—in your own time too—on my 'broidery curtains.'

Mary smiled at last, a wide, frank, smile. The more she knew of her mistress, the more she valued her innate kindness and generosity. 'Thank you, mistress,' she murmured. 'I'd like to visit the market right well, and my sister Annie shall have the bonniest new girdle of plaited leather that this money will buy.'

'A girdle? Aye, a pretty gift. Silk seems softer and prettier than leather, though,' said Mrs Poynter as they were helped into the cart. 'Your Annie's got eyes as blue as the summer skies. Why not search out a sky-coloured silken girdle for her?'

Opposite them in the cart sat Dick, holding down a crate of hens for the market, and Mary saw his lips move, but could hear no word above the hens' cackling.

'What did you say, Master Dick?' she enquired.

'I ... I said that if her eyes be the colour of the sky, then yours be like the sky reflected in a quiet pool,' said Dick with a rush. 'For your eyes have the most sparkle in 'em that I've ever seen.' His face had turned beet red at his own temerity, and Mrs Poynter chuckled.

'Aye, Mary's growing up to be a pretty lass,' she said generously, and Mary thanked them both with a smile for the compliment.

The past months had given Mary a beauty she had hitherto lacked. Too small and thin for anyone to consider her handsome, she had lost her customary pallor with easier work and better living conditions and the curves of her figure showed to good advantage under the thin silk of what had once been Mrs Poynter's best plum-coloured gown and kirtle. Because she knew no fear of an undeserved beating, Mary had lost much of her timidity, laughing out loud when circumstances warranted it, and talking easily with her fellow servants and Mrs Poynter, though she still knew all the agonies of shyness when faced with strangers.

Now she fingered the kerchief of fine white lawn round her neck. A gift from an 'unknown', though Mary knew well enough it was Dick. She smiled into his eyes as he watched and saw an answering smile hover round his mouth before he turned his attention back to subduing the crate of fowl.

Time, she reflected, had changed more than her looks and figure. It had changed her feelings, too. She could no longer pretend to regard the Poynters or Dick with abhorrence. They had won her affection with their sincerity and kindness and now by the very fact that he did not press for some answering show of feeling, Dick was winning her regard. She glanced covertly at him as they cart jogged over the rough moorland road. He was very handsome, with crisply curling dark hair and he was broad in the shoulder yet narrow in the hips, so that he moved with a speed and economy of movement which Mary thought remarkable in so big a man.

Mary tried to conjure up a picture of Frank to place disparagingly alongside Dick, and found it disconcertingly easy to see him in her mind's eye—the keen glance, the urgent voice, the touch of his hand on hers were all there before her, and even beside such slight memories, the reality of Dick's presence faded into insignificance. She shifted on the hard wooden bench and thought angrily that she should stop day-dreaming, like a foolish child. She knew Dick was not only the better looking of the two, he was a better match and quite probably a better man into the bargain. He loved her, he wanted her for his wife. Tomorrow is the wedding, she told herself. When Annie makes her vows, I shall make mine. I shall vow to forget past foolishness, and Frankie Drake along with it. And I'll vow to bind my thoughts to Dick Poynter.

Her thoughts were disturbed by the cartwheels meeting the cobbled roadway as they drove into the centre of Plymouth and drew up outside the Turk's Head. Dick and his father handed down the two women, then they disappeared into the cool darkness of the taproom, leaving Mary and Mrs Poynter to wander amongst the stalls, exclaiming and fingering the goods displayed.

Mary was just about to purchase the very girdle which she was sure Annie would most covet, when Mrs Poynter said with surprise, 'Mary! Is that your brother Harry coming towards us? He must be back from his venture and have come into Plymouth like us, to buy a bride-gift. Fancy that now, and you so fond of your family. He's coming over.'

Mary turned joyously to greet Harry —and instead, saw Francis Drake staring down at her, his blue eyes blazing out of his tanned face. For a moment her heart seemed to turn over, and the stalls, the people, and the close-leaning houses executed a wild and whirling jig. Then her vision steadied, and she said calmly enough, 'Why, brother Harry, fancy you being at the market! You have returned from your adventurous voyage then. We are here—my mistress and I—to buy bride gifts for Annie, who will wed her William tomorrow. I am to be one of her attendants and sister Ruth the other.'

'Aye, home from sea, that's me,' His voice was low, a little troubled, and his eyes searched her expression hungrily. 'I'd like to talk to you, sister. Learn all the news from home. May you walk apart with me a little?'

But Mrs Poynter would not hear of such a thing. 'Shame on you, Master Newman,' she said heartily. 'You'll be seeing your sister Annie herself tonight, don't take the news secondhand when she could have the pleasure of telling you herself. And indeed, you will soon know more than Mary here for she has only been home once since she's lived with us. Tell me, what have you bought for Annie? Mary will give that silken girdle, and I've chosen the most cunning pomander, silver gilt, stuffed with sweet herbs. 'Twill hang at her girdle see? Do you think 'twill pleasure her?'

'She'll be delighted,' said Drake absently. 'As for me, I've brought her gifts—none of great moment—but all found on my journeyings. Tell me, will you go to church to see her wed?'

'Of course, I'm her attendant,' Mary said quickly. 'In the morning, brother. Will you be there?'

'Oh, where else should I be, on the day my sister goes to her betrothed? Goodbye for now, Mary; Mrs Poynter.' He sketched a quick bow and was gone, mingling with the crowds who thronged the market.

'A nice young man, and a bonny one,' said Mrs Poynter with a chuckle. 'Some maid will let her heart hop into her mouth at the wedding tomorrow, whenever she catches your brother's bright eye, and thinks of the love-games he could play.'

Mary swallowed, and laughed high and breathless. She knew now that her fate was entwined with Frank Drake's, and that tomorrow if all went well, she would have a chance of a word with him, in quietness. She would not cheapen herself by asking him to marry her, but she would find out if he still wanted her. If he did, she knew herself well enough to know that not the strongest tug of conscience would stop her scheming to go to him. She had damped the fires of her feelings with a strong enough hand these four months, certain that he would never return to her; but one glimpse of him had been enough to set the flames leaping high once more.

★ ★ ★ ★

'A fine day for a briding.' Master Poynter's

voice was loud and hearty, ringing through the warm morning air.

'Yes, Annie is certainly fortunate. And I must thank you for letting me make my bridesmaid's dress from the pearl-coloured brocade left over from Mrs Poynter's new cloak. I could never have bought such fine, rich material.'

Farmer Poynter, crimsoning, muttered that it would come in for later, no doubt, and pulled the horse to a stop outside the Newman's front door. Then he drove off again to pick up his family and take them straight to the church.

Mary trod carefully across the cobbles, very conscious of the white satin slippers on her feet and the short train which trailed over the yard. She was glad the weather had stayed fine for Annie, since this dress, the finest she was ever likely to possess, was being seen for the first time.

Indoors, the Newmans stopped their whirl of activity and gaiety long enough to exclaim over the pretty picture Mary made.

'Your gown shimmers like water,' exclaimed Kate, 'and the pretty stitching in pale colours around the neck and sleeves makes you look almost as lovely as Annie.'

'Ah, but it is Annie's special day,' laughed Mary. 'Where is she?'

She was led into Annie's room and saw her sister looking blithe and beautiful, with her long wheat-gold hair rippling down her back and ribbons of cherry and purple threaded through its rich abundance. Her gown and kirtle were carnation coloured, and worked all over with silver thread which sparkled and glistened when Annie moved.

'Annie, you're beautiful,' Mary said reverently. 'You look so happy and glowing, and your gown is a fairy thing, as if some magic had woven a beautiful silver cobweb around you, to make you look lovelier still.'

'You look toothsome yourself, little maid,' said Annie cordially. 'Kate has gathered the flowers—will you carry these? Ruth, would you go to my mother when you've finished putting that wreath on your head and make sure she looks her best?'

As soon as Ruth had left them, Annie beckoned Mary closer and lowered her voice to a whisper. 'Mary my love, as soon as Ruth and the rest of the family are out at the front of the house, getting themselves settled in the carts, you are to go out to the stables. Someone wishes to speak to you there. Keep your dress above your ankles, because the outbuildings have been neglected these past few days. If all goes according to plan you'll not be travelling to church with me, so I will kiss you now. If there is some change of plan, however, come back to me as quick as can be, so that you aren't missed. I *think* I know his mind, but men are very devious. Off with you, maid!'

Mary looked round. The sunny room was empty except for themselves, and the sounds of talk and laughter were moving towards the front of the house. She kissed Annie's glowing cheek quickly, then darted down the stairs and out into the yard, holding her skirt above her ankles as she had been bidden, glancing nervously from left to right. The stableyard was still and silent save only for the movement of a couple of stalled beasts. The horses had been taken round to the front of the house, the bustle of the wedding party departing was already audible. Dreading to hear the cry, 'where's Mary?' Mary stole swiftly across the cobbles and peeped into the dimness of the stable. A man stepped out from one of the stalls, and said in a voice made harsh by emotion, 'Come inside, out of the sunshine. Mary, my darling, how beautiful you look!'

'What is happening, Frank? Will you take me to church? There is little time to talk,' begged Mary anxiously. 'Annie will do her best, but someone may notice I'm missing even now.'

'That's all right, love. Annie will say

you're following with a friend in a donkey cart. I'll take you to church.'

He led the way through the back of the stable to the shippon where a graceful chestnut mare stood, fidgetting with her long, slender legs. 'She has a pillion, so up with you,' said Drake briskly. He settled Mary comfortably, then mounted before her. 'Put your arms round me,' he ordered, 'and we'll be off for the church.'

'Couldn't we talk, first?' begged Mary, but Drake just laughed. 'Plenty of time for that later,' he exclaimed.

Soon, Mary began to enjoy the ride for its own sake. The wind caught at her hair, which was loose beneath the small filet of flowers that she wore, and tugged impatiently at the weight of it. In her nostrils the scents of the moor came gusting up, heavy with summer, and the hooves of the chestnut mare seemed scarcely to crush the grass so swiftly did she gallop. They rode through the dapple tree-shadow of small woods, and across the swift, tumbling brooks but soon, too soon for Mary, Drake slowed their steed to a more sedate pace, for they were entering a village. Mary caught the salt whiff of the sea and a tang of tarred fishing nets before she realised they were in St Budeaux.

'Why have we come here?' she murmured, scarcely caring what the answer was so long as she could ride on like this for ever, her arms tightly round her lover's waist.

'Why, we come to a wedding,' said Drake in a surprised voice. 'Here is the church.' He swung himself carefully off the sidling, dancing mare and held out his arms to Mary. She jumped into them gladly but remarked with a chuckle, 'You've come to the wrong church for a wedding, sir. Our Annie is to be wed at St Andrews, in Plymouth.'

'Who spoke of Annie's wedding? This, my girl, will be *our* wedding—yours and mine. Your brother Harry is here ahead of us to speak for you. Come on now, no holding back, eh?'

'*Our* wedding? You can't mean it!' gasped Mary, as she was pulled up to the open doorway of the small, newly built church.

'Why, sweetheart? Are you unwilling? In my absence did I lose your heart to good Dick Poynter?' He looked down at her, his eyes brimming with laughter and self-assurance. 'I had thought differently when I met you in the market yesterday, even though you called me brother!'

Mary said in a low voice, 'I have given my love to no one but you, sir. But marriage ... what will my parents say? And the Poynters? They have been good to me even though I could not love their son.'

'They can say little enough once we're wedded and bedded,' said Drake reassuringly. 'Come, maid, look happy! Here's Harry, and the parson. You must not appear surprised you know, or he might refuse to perform the ceremony. Come now, 'tis no fine service like your sister Annie is having, and no wedding feast either except a dinner for the three of us on the way to London.' He looked down at her anxiously. 'Mary, do you want to leave here unwed? Annie thought otherwise, but she could have been wrong.'

Mary found her voice at last. 'I'll wed you more happily than any other in the whole kingdom, Frank,' she said resolutely. 'Let them be angry if they must. I shall be with you, and care nothing for them.'

Forgotten now was Mrs Poynter's kindness, Master Poynter's reluctant generosity, and the steady flame of young Dick's devotion. She could only think of the man who held her hand so tightly, who smiled down at her with such proud possessiveness, who was leading her into the dimness of the church porch where Harry and the parson waited.

★ ★ ★ ★

'We are really married, then? I am Mistress Mary Drake?' Mary's voice held awe as she glanced from Frank to her brother Harry. They were sitting in a tavern on the road to London, eating the sustaining dinner which Frank had promised her.

Both men laughed at her timid enquiry. 'Of course you're married, sister,' Harry said teasingly. 'Wedded but not yet bedded. You'll not question your state tomorrow morning, eh, Frankie?'

Drake looked up from the close attention he had been paying to his food and smiled reassuringly at Mary. 'Come now, Harry, don't fill the wench's thoughts with the horrors ahead,' he said, whilst Harry shouted with laughter. 'Drink to our health, our future happiness, our children—and our success in all things.'

As they drank and laughed, Mary glanced surreptitiously at her brother. He was sunburned, broader in the shoulder than she remembered him, with an air of independence which he had never worn so comfortably before. Previously, she thought, his attitude had been one of defiance, but now he was aware of himself as his own master, and would not allow his father's petty spite and bullying to mean more to him than did the passing annoyance of a gnat.

She had already gazed at Drake's face as though the more she looked, the more she could become a part of him. She thought she saw in his expression a maturity which had been lacking before, and a shining light of purpose, too. But she was not so bedazzled by her new status that she believed herself to be unprejudiced. So now she said lightly, to make the men think her calm and grown-up, 'Where have you been, all these months? Did you sail to the Netherlands with the navy? If so, you were lucky to get back home so soon.'

'We've been busy,' Drake told her with a smile. 'Captain Hawkins is a good man, Mary. He delivered his reprimand but was willing to forget and forgive as soon as he realised I had learned my lesson. I shall never commit such foolishness again. As for the actual work we've been doing, it has been more in the nature of a commission from John Hawkins. Don't you worry, lass, I've money enough now to pay for our lodgings until we can settle down in a home of our own. But for a while at any rate, I shall be best away from Plymouth. There is still talk in the town of how I left men to die miserably under the lash of the Spanish Inquisition. One day I'll redeem such talk a thousandfold, but until then I have to learn my trade and you, poor little wife, will be left often alone. Do you mind?'

And Mary, even as she bit her lip to keep back reproaches, saw that minding would only make her lot harder, it would not change it. She was married to a man with a purpose which would take him always from her, always adventuring his mind and body in realms where she could not follow. She swallowed hard, and looked up at him so that he should not see how afraid she was of loneliness. 'You are a sailor, Frank, and I must learn to be a sailor's wife,' she said. But it was the right thing to say, as she saw from her brother's approving smile and Drake's patent relief, which broke from him in a crow of laughter as he squeezed her shoulders, smiling into her eyes.

'*Good* l'il maid,' he said in a broad Devon accent, then, 'Have you eaten enough? Then we will bid your brother goodbye and we'll be off. You can ride for a good few miles yet, can't you? Harry will bring your little mare round and throw you into the saddle, then we can be well on our way to London before we have to stop for the night.'

'I can eat no more,' said Mary truthfully. The thought of her new husband telling her so calmly that he would soon be leaving her had quite taken away her appetite. But once again, her remark earned her the approving glance, the fond smile. And soon she was kissing Harry goodbye, with tears, as he promised to explain everything to her parents, and to the unfortunate Poynters.

'Tell them I could never have been happy without Frank; tell them I'm sorry,' called Mary over her shoulder as Frank led her small, sturdy pony out of the yard leaving Harry waving to them from the tavern doorway. 'Give my love to Annie—oh, did she like the girdle?'

Faint on the wind came his words as the horses broke into a canter. 'She loved the girdle, sweeting, and is happy that you are both brides.'

The red dust rose under the horses' hooves and Mary waved now to a last glimpse of Harry as he was hidden by the curve in the road.

It was the last she would see of her brother or the rest of her family for some time to come.

5

ALONE AT LAST

The inn where they had spent the first
night of their marriage had welcomed
them, obviously with no idea that they
were but newly wed. They had sat down
to a good meal of rabbit pie with several
side dishes and finished off their repast
with sweetmeats and fruit. Then they had
gone to bed.

Mary woke first in the morning, when
the July sunshine discovered a chink in
the bedcurtains, and fell warmly across her
face. She stirred and opened her eyes. The
bedcurtains, richly embroidered, puzzled
her for a moment, for she was accustomed
to being roused by the dawn light falling
across her face as she lay on her straw

pallet. Swiftly, recollection flooded her. She was married! Last night she had climbed into this bed with Frank and despite her resolve, she had been shy and afraid; but they had grown tender in the close, warm intimacy of the bedclothes and her lover had found her a willing pupil in the arts of lovemaking. She smiled to herself; he knew little of women, he had told her. She did not know whether it was true or not, neither did she care very much. After their first fumbling embrace, to love had been natural, inevitable.

Now she curled catlike in the shaft of sunshine, feeling all the pulses of her body beating strongly, sure of his reaction should she wake him. But she would enjoy this sensation of being a woman grown, first. She felt the sheets, smoothing the linen between finger and thumb. Often enough she had made beds like this since she had been in service with the Poynters, yet she had never slept in one before. The pillow was soft beneath her cheek and she could scarcely refrain from a feline purr of satisfaction as she moved in the warm springy softness of the feather mattress. The little hairs on her bare arm stood up, as though alarmed, when Frank murmured her name and moved, flinging his arm across her body. She watched his face as his eyelids lifted, fluttered, then suddenly he was awake, pulling her towards him so that she felt his breath, warm and urgent, against her cheek. She saw his nostrils dilate as he felt her body move beneath him, and the lids droop over his bright blue eyes as his desire rose. As he slid his hands beneath her shoulder blades she thought with sleepy triumph, ah, he'll not talk of leaving now that he knows how sweet love can be. I shall win myself a few weeks at least to enjoy the pleasures of being a wife.

★ ★ ★ ★

'But Frank, we've only been married four

days, and you talk of going off to sea again, for Master Hawkins,' protested Mary, half laughing. 'Surely you don't mean to abandon me so soon?'

Drake smiled too, but when the smile was spent, his face was very serious. 'Mary, listen to me. This is a chance to recover myself, a chance to learn my trade, to earn some money. Every man has to work to keep his wife, and mariners are no exception. Don't think I leave you so soon willingly, my sweeting. I would rather tarry here with you for even longer. But the truth is, the Hawkins are willing to be extremely generous. I have sold the *Judith*, in order to enable me to lodge you somewhere in a fair degree of comfort. I'd like you to have a little maid to help you in the house, and a manservant to look after your horse. The voyage I make for the Hawkins will be one of discovery. We have talked long and hard, and one thing is essential. The coast of the Americas must be explored, the natives befriended. It is only thus that we shall be able to strike at Spain, and we must strike at Spain if we are to win ourselves a share of the New World, for they will not willingly let us trade there.'

'But you made one voyage of discovery when you left me to be a hired servant to the Poynters,' grumbled Mary. 'Must another be undertaken so soon?'

'I must take what chances are offered,' Drake said firmly. 'Come now, Mary my darling, the sooner I am gone the sooner the work will be over, and I will return. Will you lodge in Plymouth, or London? I shall sail from Plymouth and return there, but London is livelier for you and what is more, you will have no fuss with your parents or the Poynters regarding your speedy and somewhat unconventional marriage.'

'I'll stay in London until you can be with me,' Mary said quickly. She knew she had paid the Poynters in poor coin for their kindness, and dreaded returning to Plymouth alone, where she might be badly thought of, and with reason. 'But you won't leave *yet*, will you, Frank?'

'I'll find you comfortable lodgings, and see to your manservant. The wench you should hire yourself,' Drake replied. 'Is there no one known to you in London? No relation who might show you the sights, perhaps take you to court?'

Mary laughed. 'Lord above, I be a zimple maid out of Devon, zur! I number as acquaintance none in this gurt zity.'

'Never mind, but 'tis as well you don't really speak with a broad accent,' Drake told her, laughing. 'For we'll rise high, together, Mary. When I've made our fortunes, you'll be a grand lady with your own carriage, and a house in Plymouth and another in London. Fine clothes you'll wear, my love, and diamonds will cluster at your throat. But until then, I will try to find you a reliable manservant, and I'll speak to a friend who will maybe introduce me to a woman of good birth to keep an eye on you.'

He was as good as his word. Within a week Mary was ensconced in her first home. She had the basement part of a handsome house in a quiet, tree-lined street. Drake had chosen that particular house on the advice of another tenant, a Mrs Amy Shelton who was a relative of the ill-fated Boleyns and therefore of the Queen, so that she was sometimes at court. Mary had been very nervous and afraid of meeting with such an illustrious person but her fears were soon proved groundless. Amy Shelton was a friendly, talkative woman, frankly middle-class, the wife of a prosperous merchant. She took an instant liking to Mary, offering to find her a manservant who was both clean and honest. 'For your little wife is young, and ignorant of such matters,' she said severely to Drake. 'She should be with her friends and relations if you are to leave her, and not alone in this hard-hearted city.'

Drake, who had no desire to explain that he had virtually stolen his bride from under her mother's nose, said stiffly, 'She prefers to be in London, mistress. But I would be grateful if you would look to her welfare whenever your time permits, for as you say she is young—she won't be sixteen for a couple of months yet.'

So everything was arranged satisfactorily. The maid-servant chosen by Mrs Shelton was a pretty, practical child of fourteen, who despite her lack of years and inches was far worldlier and more knowing than her mistress. 'Living in London as I've done all my life, you either grow knowing or die young,' she said frankly. 'I'm sharp and healthy, which is how I've survived. Orphaned I am, but I served as a kitchen wench in the Shelton's town house from the time I was eight, so I know a thing or two. But when the mistress told me you needed a wench, I knew it was my chance to better myself.' She turned her bright gaze on Mary. 'My name's

Becky, Mistress Mary. And I'm a love-child which should go without saying, seeing as how if I'd been 'spectable, I'd have been kept by my family. Pretty enough, aren't I?' Mary laughed, and admitted that Becky was extremely pretty. 'Well, my looks will get me a husband, if I can save enough of the money you pay me to give myself a dowry,' said Becky practically. 'For pretty or not, there are few men who will take on a penniless orphan bride.'

'I know of such a man,' Mary said softly to herself.

When the time came for Drake to begin his ride down to Plymouth to join his ship, he was relieved to find that his wife did not weep or try to persuade him to change his mind.

'Write to me,' she urged him. 'Send me letters back whenever you meet a homecoming vessel. Kind Mrs Shelton will read them to me.'

'I'll write,' promised Drake, giving her

a hug. 'How will you employ your time when I'm gone?'

'You'll discover that when you get back,' Mary said provocatively. 'Perhaps curiosity will bring you home the sooner.'

He rode away soon after, comfortably aware that this time, his return would not be a matter of indifference but that he would be eagerly awaited, and that for his part, the return would not be to an inn or tavern with a bored host waiting on him but to his own house, with a wife who would regard his comfort as her first concern. It was a pleasant thought for one who had been lonely for many years now, and lessened the hurt of his first parting.

As soon as her husband was out of sight, Mary returned to her lodgings. She had a parlour, sparsely furnished, and behind that a kitchen where a fire kept the ovens hot even on a warm, moist August day like today. Above stairs she had a principal bedroom with the little cupboard leading off it where her maid would sleep when Frank was home. Whilst he was at sea, Becky should share the larger, airier chamber. The stables at the back of the house were shared by all the tenants, but Mary felt rich, remembering the stall with the dun pony eating hay, and the tiny room above it where her man, Job, slept and ate.

She went into the parlour and sat down before the open window. Frank had gone, she did not know when he would return. His expedition was most secret, she knew little other than that he was sailing a ship called the *Swan,* commanding her and her sister ship, the *Dragon.* Both were small, she had gathered that much, so the men needed to crew them would be few, and Frank said that men would wish to voyage with him. Her brother Harry would not sail this time since he was courting a pretty Plymouth wench who did not take kindly to being left when her swain could find work in plenty on the surrounding farms.

Mary's resolve was to spend her time

until her husband's return doing two things; she would learn to read, and she would learn to be a lady. Her accent was far from pure, and she had little idea of how the great ladies of the land conducted themselves. At first she had thought she might go into service in London, but cooler and rational reasoning had convinced her of the unwisdom of that particular scheme. If her husband rose with the meteoric swiftness he seemed to expect—and she was confident that he would—then admitting to having married a kitchenmaid of one of his new acquaintances would not go down well.

She sighed, and opened the window a little wider. The warm rain fell, soft but persistent, ringing gently on the cobbles, sliding in fat drops down the glass window panes. The obvious course would be to ask Mistress Amy how she should set about learning the ways of the gentle-folk. That person, with her jolly laugh and her daringly low cut evening dresses, had already made it plain she would help all she could. Mary wondered whether Amy Shelton could teach her to read, as well. Then she heard a crash from the kitchen. Smiling, she thought of the past months, when she had been the little maid who dropped dishes, watching with helpless horror as they shattered on the tiles or pouncing on them with breathless relief if they bounced on the rushes. Now she was the mistress, and should rebuke poor Becky. Still smiling, she made her way to the kitchen.

6

LONDON LIFE

'Mary, it is quite useless!' Amy Shelton threw the book she held down on the table and put her head in her hand. 'I never was a bright child, it was all I could do to learn my letters, and it is painfully obvious that though my mother may have beaten me often, she only beat the knowledge into my head, and not sufficient wits to enable me to pass my learning on.'

'It isn't you, Amy. It is me. I must have a head full of sawdust. A *wooden* head full of sawdust,' Mary said remorsefully. 'The trouble is, all the letters look so alike to me! But I simply must learn to read before Frank's return. How I have dreamed of surprising him with my accomplishments, and now I shall lack the most important art of them all!'

'You have learned to cook, to run a house, to market, and to manage very well on a small income,' Amy reminded her. 'You could sew well and daintily before, but now you can make truly ravishing gowns, and your Devonshire accent is scarcely more than a richness of your speech!'

Mary looked at the older woman with real gratitude. 'How good you are, Amy! But can you suggest any one who could teach me to read? I do so long to learn.'

'Yes, I know a very good tutor, who teaches all manner of important people. He will spare you an hour or so each day until you have mastered reading. It won't be long, Mary, which is why I get so annoyed with myself because you have very nearly grasped it already. But there, the tutor shall have the credit for all my hard work these past months.'

'You have taught me things that I

could never have learned from another,' Mary cried hotly. 'Why, I understood nothing about the Queen of Scots and her schemings with the Duke of Norfolk, nor why such things mattered to ordinary folk until you explained them so simply and well. I even understand the significance of the rising in the North! And had it not been for your kindness, I should never have stood close to the Queen as she came back from hunting so that I could see for myself her long bright eyes, and her white skin, and her beautiful clothes. Oh, I shall never forget that day as long as I live!'

'You'll see her often enough, I daresay, when your husband returns. Judging by his letter, he is making good use of his little barks,' said Amy placidly, but her eyes softened. The girl was a good girl, and grateful for small favours.

'Yes, the letter!' said Mary, instantly diverted. 'Would you read it to me again, Amy? See, I have it here.' She produced the letter, much thumbed and creased, from the hanging purse at her waist.

'You try to read it to me,' Amy said, suddenly inspired. 'I know Frank's handwriting is not of the best, but you must know it by heart, almost.'

'His handwriting is very *grand*,' said Mary doubtfully. 'I haven't dared to handle the pages too much, for fear they'll come to pieces. But I'll try to read it, with your help.'

She spread the pages out on the table and the two women bent over the spidery, slanting handwriting. Mary began to read, falteringly at first, then with more confidence.

The letter had been written from a small harbour on the coast of Darien, unknown, Drake thought, to the Spaniard. For his wife's amusement, he had described the place in detail with its narrow harbour mouth guarded by great rocky pillars so that from the seaward side, no one would have guessed that a safe anchorage lay within. As she read his words, she saw in her mind's eye the rock-girt harbour with the white sand burning beneath the noonday sun and the ships like stranded whales drawn up for careening. She saw the men from the ships hunting for fresh meat, bartering with the friendly Indians, sitting on the beach around a big fire when the stars pricked the dark night sky, eating sucking pig and yams and drinking coconut milk. She heard the harsh cries of the tropical birds as they flew swiftly through the palm trees, their colours so vivid that they seemed scarcely real. Drake spoke of fishing from the ship's boat, casting out a line to draw it in again after only a few moments with a great rainbow hued fish kicking on the end. 'Though they be so brightly coloured and strange, their flesh is sweet,' he had written. 'Strange food though it seems now, at Christmastide, when we think of you sitting over dried ling when you have eaten your fill of roast goose. And when you pile your fire high and cluster close for warmth, here are we, bathing in the shallows in the heat of the day and clustering beneath the shade of the palms when the sun is as its height.'

The letter ended with his signature, scribbled small and neat at the end of the page.

'You read that very well, Mary,' Amy Shelton said approvingly. 'I know it is familiar to you, but you could recognise most of the words and letters, could you not?'

'Yes,' agreed Mary, 'but when I think of Frank celebrating Christmas by sitting out in the open, eating wild pig roast over a fire on the beach, it seems very strange. And now it is April, and we've had no further word.'

'You are dependent on the chance of your husband meeting a vessel which is homeward bound, and the two of them being in a position to exchange more than greetings,' Amy said wisely. 'You keep on with your reading lessons and by the time Frank returns, you'll be reading and writing as well as I, and probably better. Working hard will help to pass the time, as you've already discovered.'

But as spring gradually began to show itself even in London, Mary grew more and more restless. She was in no position, unfortunately, to take herself off to Plymouth for a few weeks, and was shrewdly aware that even if she did so, she would probably spend the time gazing out to sea from the Hoe, waiting vainly for a sight of those two small vessels which her husband commanded. As it was, she had the money Frank had given her, carefully spending week by week just enough to cover the needs of her modest household. Unlike other girls in her position, she could not go back to her mother to see spring steal over the land. She dared not. She would wait until Frank himself thought the time was ripe, then she could go with him to her parents and beg their forgiveness for her hurried secret marriage.

'I've been married a year today, Becky.' Mary's tone was languorous, for the day had only just dawned. 'Imagine, a whole year! Yet I only had a few days with my husband before he left me to go a-voyaging, and in all that time I've received only one letter.'

Becky sat up on her pallet at the foot of the big bed and stared out of round, serious eyes at the older girl. 'You should have a baby to keep you company,' she said bluntly, 'But you've been busy this year, Mistress. Soon the master will be home. I'm sure of it, and then—well, if he suggests that you live in that outlandish place you speak of and if you want me, I'll come with you. After all, you've lived in London and you've enjoyed it some of the time, haven't you? I might grow to like your Devonshire, in a sort of way.'

'Oh, I'm glad, Becky,' exclaimed Mary.

125

'But could you fetch me some water to wash with, and the shift which is airing by the kitchen fire? I must get up, and we will do our marketing early, before the streets become crowded and the air hot.'

Becky jumped out of bed and ran to pull on a working gown, slipping her feet into a pair of Mary's old slippers. She left the room and Mary, in her turn, rolled out of bed. She stood before the window, breathing the fresh, cool air of the early morning, idly scratching a fleabite on her thigh.

She was still there, in a pleasant daze, not thinking of anything in particular, when she heard a commotion on the cobbles outside. Horses were coming, and a voice called something so that the foremost rider pulled his horse to a standstill. Carefully, Mary reached for her shift, and having pulled it on, approached the window and leaned out over the sill to see what was happening. There in the street below, were three men on horseback. They were talking urgently, then one pointed away down the street and the other two wheeled their steeds about and clattered off at a canter.

The remaining rider turned his head and gazed up towards the window as though he had been conscious all the time of the interested blue eyes watching him. Mary tried to draw back, but her shift was snagged on the rough wood of the windowsill. The man laughed, and Mary looked down at him, trying to convey outraged maidenhood. The next moment she had torn herself free regardless of the rent in her shift, and was pattering barefoot down the stairs, wild with excitement. Becky came from the kitchen, looking astonished. 'Mistress, there's a man leading a horse into your stable ...' she began, then with a squeak, 'Ooh, Mistress Mary, get you behind the door! He's coming in to the kitchen and you're little better than naked!' But Mary was already at the big back door, dragging it open, so that she could fall into Drake's arms, clutching at his leather jerkin whilst tears coursed down her cheeks and she could only sob foolishly, 'You've grown a beard, my heart's darling. You look so different with a beard.'

Becky saw her Master strain the slim, flimsily clad body close to him, then tiptoed out of the kitchen, unheeded. She would put out her mistress's best taffeta gown, she thought, and by the time she had done that, the first rapture of their greeting would be over. Then she would be able to bring the cauldron of water off the kitchen fire and pour the Captain a nice warm bath.

For a moment she mused on the happiness so plainly written on the faces of the two people in the kitchen. It must be pleasant to be in love, she thought enviously. Then she went about her work.

7

PLYMOUTH AGAIN

'My dear sister, you've really got no choice. If you intend to settle down in Plymouth then you must visit our mother and father. They have grown used to your absence. If you come with me in my pony cart when next I visit them, then you've nothing to fear. Only wear your best, and speak like a lady, and they'll be too over-awed to say much!' Annie Newman, now Annie Garret, sat in Mary's small front parlour and as she always did, spoke her mind frankly.

'But Annie, they hardly ever come to Plymouth! And surely my mother will storm and reproach, and keep reminding me that the Poynters were good and kind?'

129

'Nonsense, Mary. You think yourself too important, girl! There has been bad feeling between the Poynters and the Newmans to be sure; your wages were paid over on my—or should I say, our—wedding day but when you did not come back, Farmer Poynter tried to get Father to return the money. For a few months the two families were estranged but of late, Ruth has been casting her eyes at Dick and the awkwardness has been forgotten. Now be sensible, my dear. Come with me to the farm in a week—I'll be in Plymouth then for 'tis market day and I've eggs and butter to sell—and you'll soon make amends. Better take Mother some pretty piece of town finery and Father a drop of something to warm him, and they'll welcome you with open arms.'

'Annie is right, Mary, my love,' Drake said when his sister-in-law had climbed rather awkwardly—she was pregnant—into her pony cart. 'You will need all the friends you can get, living here in Plymouth. It isn't so bad when I'm with you, and even when I sail, my friends will stand by you. The Hawkins have been very kind, have they not? William and John both? But when I leave, slipping quietly out of the Sound so that few people hear of my going, then the gossips and the spiteful may begin to try to make your life uncomfortable. If they are able to point to the fact that you're estranged from your own parents, and if the Poynters whisper of bargains broken, then your lot could be hard indeed.'

'The Poynters are good people, and I'm sure would wish to let byegones be byegones,' Mary said, 'but you are right, of course, it would only give idle tongues something to gossip over if I did not exchange visits with my parents. I'll go with Annie next week, then, to the Newman farm. Will you come with us?'

'Annie thinks it better that I should go with you on a later visit,' said Frank smugly. 'She thinks my presence might be an embarrassment to your reunion.'

Mary sniffed, but did not comment. She thought, however, that it was a typical masculine action. Her husband might be brave as a lion on the deck of his ship, or plunging ashore to treat with hostile natives, but ask him to face an irate mother-in-law, and his courage abruptly left him. Still, he had done his best for her; he was going to take her to meet his brother John, who had gone to sea whilst a youth, as had Frank. He told her about all his brothers and had promised that when he departed on his next expedition, she should meet and entertain both John Drake and an even younger brother, Joseph. Patiently, he drew her out of her shell when they visited his friends the Hawkins, so that she lost her customary shyness and talked and laughed with the best.

It was autumn, for they had not moved straight down to Plymouth; Frank had arranged to rent a house near to the sea which he so loved, and they were now not a stone's throw from Sutton Pool, the inner harbour where the great ships lay at anchor. When Mary went into the small, somewhat neglected garden at the back of the house, she could see the tall mast of her husband's ship, the *Swan,* as she rode at rest on the waves that the autumn winds had brought even to that sheltered spot.

During the week that intervened, Mary was kept busy refurbishing her finest gown, talking of court matters, practising the gossip which she would relate to her mother when she and Annie paid their visit to the farm. Drake had given her gifts for her parents; for her mother, a snow white cambric kerchief to wear round her shoulders, lavishly embroidered with Spanish work and edged with all the bright tinsel glitter that good bone lace could offer. For her father he suggested a barrel of best malmsey wine and a curiosity from his voyage, a chunk of smooth coral to use as a paperweight or perhaps just to stand on a mantelpiece.

Nevertheless, when the day came, and when Annie came to the door to call for her, Mary found herself unaccountably nervous. She said a quick farewell to Drake, who was busy poring over the charts spread all over the table, and then went resolutely out into the street and climbed into the pony cart.

'Got your gifts, maid?' asked Annie briskly, slapping the reins on the pony's neck and clicking her tongue imperiously.

'Yes, and I wish I was as certain as you are that they'll ensure me a pleasant welcome,' said Mary pettishly. 'Goodness, Annie, you saw the barrel of malmsey which Job put in the pony-cart, you didn't think I had brought it in order to refresh myself on the way, did you?'

Annie chuckled. 'You might've thought it would give you courage,' she said annoyingly. 'Goodness knows, there is enough in that barrel to give us both courage, or for Father to drown his sorrows in for a day or so!'

Mary laughed reluctantly. 'Frank wanted to be generous,' she said. 'But Richard may share the wine with Father, if he wishes. You've seen the kerchief for our mother, and I've put in lengths of silk for Kate and Ruth so that they may make themselves a skirt or trim a summery cloak.'

'Well, I'm sure the wine and the kerchief will ensure you a warm welcome from our parents; but I wouldn't like to promise that sister Ruth will be equally pleasant to you, silk or no silk,' Annie said cautiously. 'Still, you'll not mind *her*, I'll warrant. She's not forgiven you for ensnaring Frank when she had her eye on him, and she thinks herself mighty irresistible, does Ruth. Then when she had decided that she would settle for Dick Poynter he has to discover you're back in Plymouth and he goes and says he hopes you are happy with your husband because he has never forgotten you, nor ever will.'

'Why should Ruth mind Dick saying he

won't forget me?' said Mary blankly. 'It is scarcely a declaration of undying love, surely! Indeed, I shall not forget him, for a kinder man would be hard to find—save for Frank of course.'

'Ah, but Ruth took it wrong, you see,' said Annie with a chuckle. 'Thought he was using his past affection for you to keep her at bay. Never saw a girl so furious in my life.'

'Well, doubtless they can best resolve that problem themselves, for I've no part in it,' said Mary resolutely. 'All I can do is keep away from the Poynters, which I had intended anyway. But it would make me happy to see Dick and Ruth wed—whatever is the matter, Annie? If you squirm like that you'll have the cart over!'

'Nothing much. I've got a touch of cramp,' muttered Annie, and Mary saw to her consternation that her sister had suddenly turned very pale. 'Would you take the reins, Mary?'

Mary moved over and took the reins,

eyeing Annie uneasily as she did so. 'Don't you go having that baby here in this little cart,' she said threateningly. 'Nor yet at the farm, for 'twon't ease my homecoming to assist at a birthing.'

Annie smiled, but her eyes were strangely fixed, as though she was seeing something that Mary could not. 'The babe isn't due for a week yet, if I've got my dates right,' she said with forced cheerfulness. 'No doubt it is nothing more than the jolting of the pony-cart over this rough track—ouch!'

'Annie, Annie, it isn't just the track, you're going to give birth to that blessed child,' exclaimed Mary, panic stricken. 'What shall I do, girl? Where shall I drive?'

'Home, to Newmans,' Annie said, through lips suddenly pale and dry. ''tis nearer to go on than turn back. Oh Mary, I'm frightened!'

'Not so frightened as I am,' muttered Mary beneath her breath, wishing with all her heart that Frank had not backed out of the encounter with her parents. Aloud she said bracingly, 'Bear up, Annie love, we're almost there, I can see the roof from here.'

'Bear up! Be sure I won't bear down,' said Annie, with a half-hearted attempt at humour. 'Thank God the weather has not played us false; a Dartmoor fog at this moment would be the death of me.'

The last half mile of the drive was the most terrible experience of Mary's life. It was all down hill, so she had to let the pony take the gradient carefully, could not press the small, sure-footed creature to a speed which might be foolhardy. Yet before they were halfway down Annie had begun to groan, and the sweat which broke out on her brow and trickled down the sides of her face went unheeded by them both, for Mary was too busy seeing that the pony kept the cart moving as smoothly as possible, and Annie held onto the side, praying that the journey might soon be over.

At their entrance into the stableyard a lad Mary had never seen before ran out of the outbuildings and took the pony's head whilst Mary slipped and stumbled over the cobbles in her haste, calling in a high, frightened voice for her mother. Mrs Newman came to the door saying irritably, 'Well, here's a pretty pickle! You'm early, and I haven't got my best gown on yet. What's the matter, miss, that you shout out so loud and shrill?'

'Annie's in labour,' panted Mary, grasping her mother's arm urgently. 'Who is home? Who can help us? Remember, this will be her first-born and there is little that I can do, for I scarcely remember you giving birth to Kate.'

'Joss, ride into Plymouth and fetch Mrs Bright, the midwife.' Mrs Newman told the stable-lad with commendable promptness. 'Come Mary. We must fetch our Annie down from the pony-cart. We'll sit her down in parlour if we can't get her up the stairs.'

Mary, helping her mother with Annie's unwieldly body, could not help smiling to herself at the sudden broadening of her mother's accent. But she admired the coolness and practicality that she showed.

'Ruth, come downstairs and stop sulking, your sister Annie's in labour,' Mrs Newman shouted up the stairs. To Mary she said comfortingly, 'Don't look so whey-faced, girl. A first baby takes its time arriving, as I know well. Happen she'll not have the child for hours. The midwife can be here in little more than two hours, if she hurries herself.'

Ruth, wearing her best gown, came quickly into the room, her rosy face concerned. 'Annie, you foolish girl!' she said sharply, but with affection. 'Never mind, my wench, mother and I will see to you.'

Annie opened a blue eye and said firmly, 'And Mary too; she be here, too, Ruth.'

Ruth gave a jerk of her head and said, 'Aye Mary will help, no doubt.'

There followed an hour of organised confusion as the girls feverishly boiled water, tore strips from a length of linen, and soothed Annie's frightened gasps and cries. Almost without realising how it had happened, Mary found herself enveloped in a huge apron, with a pair of pattens on her feet to keep her velvet shoes clean. Then they were lugging Annie upstairs, hot with terror lest she give birth on the way, and sending Kate down to the kitchen to clean out a drawer and line it with soft linen, for the child to lie upon, when it was born.

Ruth and Mary stood one each side of the bed, and tried to help Annie as her cries and moans gradually ceased and became grunts of effort. Annie grasped the bedpost with one hand and Mary's arm with the other. Scarlet faced and undignified, she strained and jerked half a dozen times with no breath to waste in screaming now, her efforts all concentrated on expelling the child within her. Mary felt her sister's nails dig into her arm, saw

Annie draw up her legs and then the baby was ejected with such triumphant force that Mary and Ruth laughed—and laughing, found tears on their cheeks.

'Mother!' called Ruth through the open door. 'The child is born. Will you and Kate bring the water up, now.'

Annie lay quietly, watching her sisters as they washed and swaddled the child. Her eyes were bright in her pale face, and though the experience had drawn the colour from her cheeks and given her an air of frailty, she said in a surprisingly strong voice, 'God's blood, but what a business it is, to have a son! I daresay he looks like a sucking pig, but he'll improve when his hair grows. I'm fair parched, mother—is there any milk in the house?'

Mrs Newman bustled out, calling for Kate, and Mary said in a low voice to Ruth, 'Was it a boy, then?'

Ruth looked at her mockingly. 'Aye, 'tis a lad. To think that you, a married woman, should ask your poor spinster sister such a question!' and miracle of miracles, they both laughed, because Ruth was so pretty and pink cheeked that she could not expect to be a spinster for long and suddenly, the old affection, which had not died but only slept during Mary's courtship and marriage, returned with its old force, and Mary knew with great thankfulness that she would always understand and love Ruth, and they need never be estranged again.

★ ★ ★ ★

'So by and large, your visit was a success?'

Mary nodded energetically, her eyes smiling at Drake, though her mouth was full of bread and cheese. She finished the mouthful and wiped the crumbs from her lips with the back of her hand. 'Lord, but I was hungry,' she said. 'We had no time to eat, what with seeing to the baby and getting a message to Annie's husband. Then Richard brought me home before driving on to see his betrothed, and all I could think of was getting myself a bite of something before I expired!'

'Well, you've had enough bread and cheese to satisfy you for a bit, I should think,' said Drake with a smile. 'Tell me about the child—and Annie. Is she well?'

'Well enough. She is going to call the boy Barnabas, after her father-in-law. He's a lovely baby, Frank, not a bit like a sucking pig, which is what Annie kept calling him. He's round and pink, with the bluest eyes; no hair to mention, just some fluff on his skull.' She gazed wistfully at her husband. 'Frank we've been wed as long as Annie and William. I know 'tis not a matter we can settle by wishing, but I *do* wish for a child. A little son of my own, with skin as soft, no, softer than the finest silk, and his little head covered with velvet. I'm old enough to take care of such a child,

Frank, when you go off to sea without me. Indeed it would be good for me, so Becky thinks.'

'Though we've been wed as long as Annie and William, we haven't been much together,' Frank said comfortingly. 'We'll have our son yet, Mary, don't you fret. He'll be as welcome to me as he will be to you, for I feel the desire for a child of my own, as do all men. But there is talk of a voyage; I would be Admiral of two ships, and it is not a chance to be lightly tossed aside, even though it may mean, perhaps that we shall not have our son for a while longer.'

'Another voyage?'

'Yes, love. To the coast which I have spent so much time exploring these past months. This voyage, Mary, will bring us fame and fortune at last!'

But to Mary, it only meant that she would be alone again; and that this time, she would hunger not only for the touch of Frank's lips on hers, and his body pressing her close. She would hunger for the imagined feel of a child in her arms, a child who would look to her for the love and attention which she had to spare, when Frank was away.

But she did not mention the matter again. Instead, she asked 'What manner of voyage will this be then, love? Will you seek for gold, or trade for slaves?'

'Not at once; no. First we must get to know the waters of the Americas as well as we know the Narrow Seas. But in time, this will lead to better things, believe me. We have to learn our lessons in seamanship and navigation first, however.'

Mary, smiling her agreement, thought that the lessons she would learn, alone in Plymouth, would be harder. She would have to learn to be self-reliant, and self-sufficient. She would have to subdue her natural desires for a child, for the company of the man she loved, even. But she had known this to be so when she married Frank; it was too late now to repine, or want to change him.

Instead she said with an appearance of complacency at last, 'When do you leave us then, my love?'

8

Although the month of May was well advanced, the soft, misty rain fell like an enveloping garment on Mary as she stepped out of the house in Looe Street, and walked a short way down the road, stepping carefully to avoid the great glinting puddles which had already formed in every hollow. Mary glanced hopefully towards the harbour but no broad-shouldered figure hurried up to meet her, apologising because he was late for dinner once again. She sighed impatiently. She knew Frank was down there, on board his ship, checking for the thousandth time that the supplies, gear and equipment which he needed were safely stowed on board his vessels. For this was not merely a voyage of exploration and discovery, carried out in great secret, as his previous two enterprises had been; this was the real thing at last. Drake was to go as Admiral of the expedition and Captain of the *Pasha,* and his brother John would command the *Swan.* Previously Frank had captained the *Swan* himself, so he knew her to be a reliable, seaworthy vessel, though only twenty-five tons. The *Pasha* was seventy tons, and Mary knew her good qualities as well as any man who would sail in her, for Frank sang the praises of this, his first flag ship, constantly.

'Seventy-three men, we will carry in all, and not one pressed; every man and boy aboard a volunteer.' The words had been said over and over, until Mary thought sometimes that she must mutter them in her sleep. And now, all they waited for was the wind. The right wind, neither too strong nor too small, but sufficient to send them sailing quietly out of Plymouth Sound before any one began to wonder where they were going, or why they were so well equipped.

Mary had walked right onto the quay of Sutton Pool now, and she stood uncertainly beneath the bows of the *Pasha,* wondering whether she should climb aboard and drag her husband forcibly back to his home. After all, with this smoky rain falling and spreading its damp and mysterious mist over land and sea so that not a breath of wind sang in the rigging, there was nothing anyone could do aboard the ships. He might just as well come and be sociable with her visitors as get his death of cold on the deck of a motionless vessel.

'Frank! Can you hear me?' she called into the listening silence. No sound answered her, only the faint lapping of the water against the harbour wall, the creaking of the masts and the slow plop! as rainwater gathered and fell. The quay was deserted for once, except for a couple of hunched and dejected gulls which perched on a pile of crates, hoping for scraps when the fishermen rowed into harbour as dusk fell.

She waited for a moment, hoping that Frank would appear, or that one of his crew would wander down to the waterside so that she could find a messenger, but no one appeared. Mary thought wryly that probably with the exception of Frank and herself, the good people of Plymouth were all indoors, enjoying their Sunday dinner, and if she intended to feed her husband a hot meal, she had better go aboard the *Pasha* herself.

Before she could change her mind, she had climbed onto the deck, awash with the gentle rain, and swung herself down the companionway leading to the Master's cabin. She opened the door softly, and there was Frank, sitting at his table with his charts spread out in front of him. His head was bent and he did not move as she entered. For a moment her heart stopped beating, then she gasped with relief. He was asleep! Worn out by days of preparation, by being constantly alert and ready to sail, he had actually fallen asleep over his beloved charts. Smiling again, she moved forward and touched his sleeve.

He woke instantly, and was instantly apologetic. 'Mary, my love, it is too bad of me,' he said, getting slowly to his feet. 'But I must plead exhaustion. Is your dinner spoiled? What will our guests think of me?'

'They're lucky to be seeing you today at all,' said Mary, instantly defensive. 'Had the wind been right, you would have sailed by now. But there, love, William Garret comes from a family who go to sea, though he is content to farm his land; he will understand. And Annie won't smother you with reproaches. Though she is a farmer's wife, her husband commands but four men; he isn't in *your* position.'

The militancy in her tone was not lost on Drake, who laughed. 'Could you be prejudiced, love?' he said lightly. 'God, wench, I pine to be off, yet I hate to leave you again. Still, no time for reproaching myself now, I have neglected our guests long enough; let me help you onto the quayside.'

They made their way back to their own front door, Mary's hand resting lightly on her husband's sleeve to keep her balance over the slippery cobbles. By the time they reached their front steps Drake's curls were diamonded with rain drops and Mary's skin gleamed like fine porcelain. But they were late, and could not waste time in prinking whilst their guests waited. 'Serve dinner at once, please, Becky,' Mary said to the maid who was hovering in the hall.

They went into the dining room and Mary said 'Sorry I've been so long, but I had to go down to the ship to remind Frank it was dinner time. Are you starving, Barney?'

Annie's son was now an imp of two, who wore his petticoats with a dashing air, and loved to swagger down to Sutton Pool with his adored Uncle Frank to inspect the big ships lying at anchor there. His small sister, Mariana, was a thriving baby of eight months, already beginning to crawl, though today she had been left at home with her nursemaid. And Mary suspected from Annie's straining breasts that her sister was pregnant once again, though no one had mentioned the fact.

A baby a year, and she looks marvellous, thought Mary enviously, eyeing her sister's roses and cream complexion and the deft way she lifted Barney onto a stool, wrapped a napkin round his neck to protect his frock, and slapped his inquisitive fingers away from the table knives all in one smooth movement. She's wonderful with her children; but then I would be as well, because I love babies, her thoughts continued. She smiled at Barney, wriggling on his stool, eyeing the preparations for the meal with excitement. 'Come and sit by me, Master Barney, and you can tell me about your farm whilst you eat your chicken broth,' she said lovingly.

Master Barney pouted ungratefully, however. 'Don' *wanna* sit by you, wanna sit by Uncle Frank,' he said, and Drake, who was fond of the little chap, said, 'Hand him over here then, Annie. I'll see to it that he doesn't mire his new frock, won't I, young man?'

They settled themselves into their seats as Becky and the kitchen maid began to bring in the dinner.

'Boiled fowl with leeks and carrots,' Drake said encouragingly to his nephew. 'Now you could make a fine mess of your front with *that*, Barney. I'll tie that napkin closer to your chin.'

'There's a leg of mutton, with a very tasty parsley sauce,' Becky said proudly, setting down another dish. 'And a fine mess of fresh green peas to go with it. And after you've done with the meat, we're serving a nice turbot with a shrimp sauce, flanked by young marrows.'

When the girl had left the room Mary said guiltily, 'Annie, you'll think I am teaching my servants badly indeed! But Becky is so proud to put a company dinner before us, knowing that she only has the kitchen maid to help her cook it at the moment. I know how well you eat at the farm, so we shall be offering you nothing unusual.'

''Tis unusual that I haven't had the burden of the cooking, for one thing,' said Annie frankly, squaring her elbows and beginning to eat heartily from a plate well heaped with food. 'Your Becky has a way with victuals, Mary. Where did she learn fancy glazing of cold meats, and which tasty sauce to serve with meat or fish?'

'She goes round to the Hawkins' house, and works in the kitchens when they're entertaining, in return for lessons from their cook,' said Mary, giggling. 'Oh, but the Hawkins have been good to us, Annie! When Frank goes off on this voyage he will leave me for longer probably, than he has done before; but it won't seem as bad as it did at first, because I shall have you within easy reach, and the Hawkins right on my doorstep. I find them practical, friendly people, and they are quite willing to help me in all sorts of ways. Mrs Hawkins will teach me how to run a great house, and then when we are rich from Frank's endeavours, I shall not be *quite* lost amidst all the grand people!'

Talking and laughing, the afternoon seemed to fly, and soon William Garret was saying he must fetch the pony-cart, for he had to be back at the farm in time to see that the beasts were fed and watered properly before being stabled for the night. Mary and Frank stood on their doorstep in the last cool grey light of evening and waved them off, then they went indoors and Mary started for the kitchen to make sure that Becky, and Prue the kitchenmaid, were managing all right without her. But Drake held her back.

'Look, love! Through the window you can see the night coming, in darker clouds. But they are moving fast for mere darkness.

This *is* cloud, and it is being driven by a wind, my darling. I tell you, we'll have all the breeze we need tomorrow! We must go to bed now, for I shall be up betimes. We'll sail at dawn, Mary!'

★ ★ ★ ★

Next morning, when Mary awoke, Drake was already out of bed, gathering his belongings in the primrose light of sunrise. Mary could see through the window a tree whose summer foliage was being stirred by a brisk breeze, and she knew that down in the Sound, the little waves would be building up, and further out to sea, the white horses would be galloping. She rolled out of bed saying softly, 'Why didn't you wake me, Frank?'

'I should have done so shortly, but I have only been out of bed a short while, myself. Come quietly down to the kitchen, and I'll rouse Job and send him to wake my brothers, if they still slumber. The men will come soon enough, but John and I, being in command, should get on board as soon as possible. As for Joseph, you've enjoyed his company I know so perhaps he can help you until we need him.'

Mary agreed gladly. She had been happy to entertain Joseph, a lad of fourteen, and he slept in their spare room now, with John Drake, who was twenty-two. The two had been in Plymouth for several months, coming and going, and Joseph had become quite a household favourite, with Becky laughingly catering for his enormous young appetite.

In a remarkably short space of time, or so it seemed to Mary, she and Becky were on the quay. They waved to the small vessels as they moved slowly out of the shelter of the harbour, watching them stagger and then recover as they met the full force of the wind and were manoeuvred to use it to advantage.

Eager to see how the ships met the open sea, Mary and Becky picked up their skirts and ran round the headland until the white cliffs of the Hoe were before them. Then they stood, eyes streaming from the force of the wind, watching the vessels ride the long Atlantic rollers.

'Home now, Becky,' Mary said at last. 'They can no longer see us, you may be sure, even if they have time to gaze back at land, which I'll warrant they have not! With a wind like this, they'll have their work cut out to keep the sails trimmed.'

The two young women turned and walked back towards the house, and Mary mused on how unobtrusively the craft had slipped out of Sutton Pool unnoticed it seemed, by any one but themselves. Then she remembered the other watchers on the quay and smiled. They had not been the only women saying farewell to their men, but with seventy-three men and boys, only one of whom had reached the age of thirty, there had not been the usual number of keening wives and wide-eyed children.

Young adventurers! Mary envied them

with all her heart as she sought her own familiar parlour. They would see things she had never seen, experience hardships she could never guess at; yet she would have given a great deal to share with them the months of trial and excitement which lay ahead.

* * * *

'We left Plymouth on the 24th May last year, yet here it is the last day of May 1573, and still we have not found ourselves the fortune we desire. This attempt *must* succeed—*shall* succeed.'

Drake was speaking earnestly to John Oxenham, as they sat well hidden on the heights above Nombre de Dios.

'It must indeed,' Oxenham replied. 'But you've won the hearts of your men to such an extent, Drake, that they'd follow you for another year if it pleased you, with only the hope of adventure ahead.'

Drake grunted, and lowering himself

onto his stomach, peered through the thin screen of jungle growth which separated them from the road leading down into Nombre de Dios. 'Well, at least if this venture—when this venture—is successful, we shall shake off Tetu,' he said rather resentfully. 'He may be a Huguenot, a Protestant insofar as a Frenchman can be such a thing, but I'd not have wished for his company. He had done nothing like the work which our company have performed, so I was reluctant, but how could I refuse him when he begged to join our venture?'

'I suppose you mean when he spoke of the horrors of St Bartholomew's Eve, last August, when the Catholic French fell upon the Protestants, and massacred them. Yes, in view of the terrors from which he and his comrades fled, you had to let him join us.'

'A pox on *that*,' Drake said frankly. 'It was the size of his ship and the number of his men that persuaded me to let him join! Why, man, we've lost so many from fever and similar ills that we could not afford to start a fight with seventy healthy Frenchmen. Still, the damage is done. Now we must make the best of it and show these Frenchies what we're worth, which is twice what they are. You've got the lie of the land fixed in your mind?'

'Aye; and it will be there for many a year after the way you've dinned the scheme into my head,' Oxenham said, grinning, but Drake was serious. 'Remember, this is our second attempt to seize the gold train from Panama,' he said. 'Our first attempt failed, not because it was badly conceived or carried out, but because a drunken fool was allowed to go unnoticed amongst us, until he grew overbold and unwary with the power of the drink and gave the alarm so that even a Spanish muleteer realised something was amiss. Yet when sober, he is a good and God-fearing fellow. So this time there must be no such occurrence. Everything has been planned down to the last detail. Are you ready? If so, we'll make our way back to the main body of the men.'

So through the long hours of the night the men lay motionless on the ground, heedless of the hard earth and insects which plagued them. Their only thought was that which Drake had voiced to Oxenham—they were being given a second chance, a thing granted to few men—and this time, they must not fail.

At last, in the darkest hour before the dawn, they heard the jangle of the mulebells as the small beasts came out of the town, bringing King Philip's treasure upon their backs. Suspecting nothing, they brought their armed escort into the very midst of the English ambush so that the man picked for the job was able to step forward and give the order to halt to the foremost and hindmost mules in the train. Drake's friends, the native Cimarroons, had told him that the mules were obedient, and so it proved, for although the men were soon busy answering the volley of bullets from the guards who accompanied the gold, Drake had to smile at the neat little beasts of burden, lying quietly chewing the tough jungle grass as dawn broke, whilst the fight raged about their long ears.

Soon enough, the Spaniards decided they were outnumbered and fled, leaving the excited English and their French allies to lead themselves with all the gold, hide the silver in convenient holes made by the giant land-crabs which abounded near Nombre de Dios, and hurry off into the jungle, hoping they would not be followed.

At least we are secure in the knowledge that the Cimarroons will not use their fantastic tracking abilities to bring their masters down on us, thought Drake, as he trudged along. The Spaniards had treated the natives with such bestial and unreasonable cruelty that it had been an easy matter for Drake to persuade them to assist his venture since it would damage the hated conquerors.

The French Captain, Tetu, had been badly wounded in the skirmish and presently he and two of his men dropped behind. But the others hurried on as best they could, carrying the precious burden that meant their voyage had been a success, and England should be proud of them. The march back to the pinnaces with the gold burdening them, however, soon became a nightmare with thick jungle growth which had to be cut down before they could continue their journey and tropical storms and gales which burst upon them with unprecedented violence. Worst perhaps of all, were the sensations of burning danger at their backs should they be pursued, and the fear that their pinnaces might have been discovered by the Spanish, for they had not realised that carrying the gold would slow their progress as much as it had done. Therefore, the boats which had arranged to rendezvous with them at the river mouth would be cruising aimlessly, at the mercy of any passing Spaniard who happened to spy them.

Because of this, rests were short—and so were rations. But the men did not grumble. They had not much idea of the worth of the gold they carried, but they knew it exceeded their wildest dreams. Used to the hard life at sea, this additional hardship seemed worth suffering, because of the reward that they carried on their backs. So the last night of their trek they stayed for neither rest nor food, but trudged doggedly on through the wildest and wickedest storm that any of them had known, whilst rain lashed at their faces and lightning played amongst the gale-torn tree tops.

They reached the river as dawn was breaking, and the glint of water through the trees ahead was like a glimpse of the promised land. 'Softly, boys,' Drake ordered in a croak so harsh it scarcely sounded like his own voice. 'Don't burst out of the shelter of the trees until I've made sure our boats await us.'

It was then that their aching, burning eyes, robbed of sleep for so long, saw the dreaded sight. Instead of their own pinnaces they saw seven Spanish longboats, manned by Spaniards who talked and gesticulated loudly.

'They must have captured our pinnaces,' muttered Oxenham softly. 'They'll know the frigate is bound to be near at hand; they'll be after her next, I'll be bound.'

'Our men would not tell so much so lightly,' Drake said boldly, though despair hung round his heart like a fog. 'Let us wait in the shelter of the trees and see what these Spanish pigs do next.'

And next, to the great puzzlement of the English, the longboats gathered together as the sun broke through the still heavy clouds overhead, and made for the open sea.

'We're not much better off for their absence,' said a sailor glumly. 'We've the treasure of the King of Spain on our backs, but we can do nought with it here except to let it burden us down with its weight until we sink into the soil and the land crabs gnaw the flesh from our bones.'

Drake eyed the man with a certain sympathy but said at once, 'Nonsense! I said before, our men in the pinnaces would not give us up so easily. And did you see one prisoner aboard the longboats? I'll wager that if our lads are captured—and I say *if* mind—they will be taken to a Spanish prison before they would talk. As for despair, why should we despair, when the frigate is lying off the coast, waiting for us? We could go to it by land but that would take time; what is to stop us going by sea?'

Several things, such as no boats, thought John Oxenham with wry humour, but he did not speak aloud. The faces of the men as they gazed at their leader were trusting, full of hope once more. Drake said briskly, 'Now my plan is this. The storm has brought down some mighty timbers from higher up in the forest; see where they have been cast up on the beach? When I was a lad I often made a clumsy raft, and sailed it on the tide-water. We could build us a raft from those tree trunks, and I will engage to sail her with anyone who will accompany me to where our ship is moored, and will bring back transport and succour to the rest of you if we have to fight every Spaniard in the Indies.'

And John Oxenham, who believed in his heart that such a venture was impossible, quite mad, found himself working side by side with his companions, urging them to greater effort, cheering them with talk of what they would do with their share of the gold, until after only a few hours work, the raft stood ready to take to sea.

'We'll rig a biscuit bag for a sail,' Drake said with great good-humour, duly slitting the bag open and hanging it from the makeshift mast. 'Now who will sail with me in this stout vessel, to bring aid to our countrymen?' He rather spoilt his show of confidence in the 'stout vessel' by adding hastily, 'I think all volunteers must be strong swimmers.'

'I swim like a fish—or like the frog you call us when you t'ink we are not listening,' boasted one of the Frenchmen, his dark beady eyes twinkling. 'I'll come wit' you, Captain.'

'And I,' said another of the French sailors quickly, 'I swim like my compatriot here, and would razzer share a ducking wiz a Drake, than see a Spaniard smile!' The men laughed, and applauded the pun, and John Smith, who had already climbed aboard the raft and was now standing knee deep in water to help push her off, said merrily, 'The Cap'n knows I've been swimmin' as long as 'ee, so let us be off.'

But once clear of the land, the perilous ride on the raft was no laughing matter. The logs rubbed together, so there was always a fear that part of one's person might get nipped between the moving trunks, and the sea was so rough they were continually finding that the waves broke right over them. Soon, all four men gave up the unequal struggle to stand upright. It was far too perilous. 'Kneeling is safer, and also more appropriate,' Drake said with a laugh, and had to clutch at the slippery rope as a wave buffeted them, filling his mouth with bitter salt water so that he coughed and spluttered. Later still, the sun, which was now high in the heavens, began to make itself felt on their salt-wet skin. 'Like a porker I feel, being salted alive and turned into bacon,' groaned John Smith. Yet still the mood of mad adventure was so strong on them that his companions laughed through cracked lips.

'We're making good headway, Captain Drake, sir,' remarked Pierre. 'A pleasure cruise t'is may not be, for my t'irst is strong, but I swear you could teach us to build a craft sufficient to get us home, if all else failed.'

'The idea hadn't occurred to me, but in the event ...' began Drake, when a yell from John Smith brought them all to their feet, scanning the sea with desperate eagerness. 'Pinnaces, our two pinnaces!' Smith shouted hoarsely, executing a clumsy jig and all but tumbling into the sea. 'Give 'em a shout, boys, for we're so low in the water that they'll not see us.'

Shout they did, but the sun was low in the sky now, and with dusk creeping over the water, there was little chance of the crews of the pinnaces seeing the flat raft bobbing on the waves. With deepening despair the men saw the pinnaces slide out of sight behind the headland. But Drake was not deterred. 'They've run for the lee shore because night is coming down,' he said exultantly. 'Come, lads, trim our sail and turn her for this side of the headland. We'll abandon the *Jolly Last Hope* and march round to find out just what those sailors have been doing. And why they weren't at their stations this morning when we came to the end of the jungle.'

''Twas a good thing they wasn't, sir,' remarked Smith. 'Seein' as them Spaniards would have given 'em a nasty sort of reception.' But after that they were too busy guiding the wayward raft to shore to bandy words about their companions.

'Are you certain it is your own pinnace, Captain?' Pierre said, suddenly anxious. 'When I t'ink back, we were a good way from your men, and zey were moving away from us.'

'Lord, yes. One was my own pinnace, The *Minion*, which I'd know anywhere. Would not you, Smith?' The other Englishman murmured a fervent assent as they dragged the raft up on the beach in the gathering dusk and hastily flung some seaweed over her, to hide her from prying eyes. Almost in silence, they jogtrotted through the belt of jungle which separated them from the other side of the headland until they saw ahead of them a lightening in the trees which meant that they were about to emerge onto the other beach.

'When we get out of the trees, run as if we were being pursued,' Drake commanded them, his eyes twinkling. 'We must pay them out for the fright they gave us this morning! We'll pretend we are all that is left of the landing party and that we have been chased off the treasure like thieving dogs. Come now, start running.'

Entering into the spirit of the joke, the men ran out of the trees like hares, tired though they were. The sailors, having scarcely drawn their boats up on the sandy shore, took in the position—or so they thought—and immediately dragged the captain and his companions into a pinnace and rowed away from the dangers of the imagined pursuit.

'What happened? How came you here? Where are the rest of the landing party?' The questions came thick and fast, but

Drake only looked glum and replied 'Well,' in his most sarcastic tone.

'We couldn't be at the meeting place by the hour appointed, for a gale blew us off course, but nothing would have stopped us other than the hand of God stirring the weather,' a young sailor explained, almost in tears. 'Ah, but the loss of the treasure is nothing, 'tis the loss of the brave men who adventured with you that will strike us sore.'

Drake, unable to keep the good news to himself a moment longer, snatched from inside his doublet an ingot of gold, and swinging it in a wide arc so that the men in both boats could see it clearly, despite the greyness of the evening light, he said, 'What have we here, eh? I may have told you wrong. It seems that some of the Spanish gold has stuck to *my* fingers, at any rate, and I daresay the lads you fear dead will be guarding your share of the gold for you, on the river bank where we had intended meeting.'

There was a moment of incredulous silence before the man who had first spoken said tentatively, 'Guarding ...? Gold ...? You mean all did not end in disaster for you? The capture of the mule train went as planned? Captain, we would never linger when you needed us, but we had no choice this morning. By God, you've made our fortunes!'

''Twas as well you didn't come this morning, lad,' John Smith said kindly. 'For when we reached the meeting place, there were seven Spanish longboats lying in the mouth of the river. We thought for certain you'd been captured, and we set out in a raft ...'

When the story of their adventures and the perilous voyage had been told, the man in charge of the pinnaces said, 'We've been rowing round the headland, Captain, but as darkness is falling so rapidly, should we not return to the *Pasha?* We could pick the remainder of the crew up in the morning, seeing as how you've been through some bad times already today.'

But Drake would not hear of it. 'I swore to those lads that I'd bring them aid, and that's what I intend to do,' he said firmly. 'Besides, they are as tired and as wet as we, and they have the fear of the Spaniards also. No, we must go back, and bring aboard every man and every last ingot of gold. It may have to be done by moonlight, or torchlight, but it must be done at once.'

So, rowing in the teeth of the strong wind, the men laboured at their oars, Drake as hard as any. They reached their companions before dawn, and such was the belief in their leader held by every man under his command, that he was greeted cheerfully and gladly, but not one member of the stranded expedition expressed a word of surprise!

At that early hour, after two sleepless nights, the men had to work until they were dropping, to load every last ounce of the precious gold aboard and then the pinnaces were rowed out of the mouth of the river into a heavy sea. But the talk, the laughter, the sheer *gladness* because they had succeeded, they were alive and would be rich, was so strong in the men that it could almost be seen.

By the time they sighted the *Pasha* and their French companion, it was full daylight, and stiff, sore, and exhausted though they were, they began the task of hauling their gold and themselves aboard without delay. But there was to be no rest for them yet. Drake insisted that before a meal was taken or anyone fell asleep, the treasure should be equally divided between his own crew and the Frenchmen, not forgetting a share for Captain Tetu and his comrades, who had not caught up with the shore party in time to be lifted off. When that had been done, and only then, he went down to his cabin to lie drowned in sleep throughout the day and the following night, until he awoke on the morning of 8th June with a ravenous hunger and

179

thirst, which was quite unable to stifle the well-being which coursed through his body every time he thought of their return home.

9

SUNDAY SERMON

Mary sat, quiet and attentive, in her pew at St Andrews, but her mind was not on the sermon. As usual, her imagination played with the picture that was nearest her heart—the return of the *Pasha* and the *Swan*, with her husband triumphant upon the deck. That the ships might return without him was not a thought she would allow to bruise her mind, nor did she like to envisage his return without the fortune he had promised. Mary was not greedy; she had no desire for the gold for herself. But she knew that to Drake, success was measured in the men he brought safely home, and the gold they brought with them.

So she sat in the filtered morning sunshine, and prayed for her man.

As the service took its course, she sank back onto her seat and chided herself for not listening to the sermon; it was a good sermon, but something outside the church kept clutching at her attention. There were small noises drifting up the hill on the breeze, noises from the harbour, like ... like ...

She realised by the stirring and muttering coming from all around her that she was not the only person in the church who found it difficult to give proper attention to the parson. Others in the congregation had men at sea, and no one, from the highest to the lowest, could foretell when the small barks and frigates would come nosing into the harbour, or what tidings of their loved ones would be brought.

Suddenly, an impulse stronger and older than herself brought Mary to her feet. Heedless of the startled eyes of her fellow worshippers, of the concerned face of the preacher, she walked as quickly as she could down the aisle and left the church. As soon as she was outside in the August sunshine, she could feel the pull of the harbour as though she were a pin being drawn to a magnet. Her heart felt absurdly light, as light as her feet as she began to run down towards the ships she could see rocking lightly alongside the quay. For a moment, as the vessels came into plain view before disappearing behind the houses, her heart misgave her. They were not the *Pasha* and the *Swan*. She had not waited so long nor watched so constantly for *those* vessels. But the intuition which told her that Drake awaited her was stronger even than the commonsense of what she could see with her own eyes. She ran faster, unaware that as she left it, the church had emptied behind her, and that now at her heels, running more slowly but with no less enthusiasm, was the entire congregation of St Andrews.

183

She emerged from the shadows of Pike Street right onto the quay itself, her breath short in her throat at the unaccustomed exercise. The harbour seemed to smile in the sunshine. The fishing boats had spread their nets, the gulls hovered and called, yet the Sunday peace had vanished as though today were market day. Everywhere men staggered comically, calling to each other and to the people who had not been held up by the long chase from St Andrews to the harbour. Mary's eyes went from one tanned face to another, but before she could even begin to worry or wonder, she found herself caught up and pressed hard against a soft, velvet doublet which she certainly did not recognise.

But not even unfamiliar Spanish style clothes could hide the well-remembered shape of Frank's shoulders or the familiar feel of his hands on her back and when she tilted her head she saw his eyes, looking bluer than ever, twinkling down at her. 'Oh my heart's darling, you're safe! How well you look!' Mary said breathlessly, putting her arms round his neck and rubbing the short, crisp curls at the back of his head. 'You've been away so long, yet you've scarcely changed at all.'

'You have, you're prettier than ever,' Drake said, gazing down at her small face, rosy now with delight and the surprise of seeing him. 'My, how you ran out onto the quayside, my little love! Like a wild kitten chasing the autumn wind!'

'I was in church,' said Mary, remembering. 'And I got the strangest feeling. I was suddenly absolutely certain that I ought to be down here at Sutton Pool. Gracious, the sermon had only just begun, but it was as though I was being led from the building to where I *should* have been. And when I saw the ships I knew they weren't yours, yet still the feeling urged my feet to fly faster.'

'The ships are mine, by right of conquest if nothing else,' Drake said, grinning. 'And we have brought back gold—gold—gold!

England has seen nothing like it; the treasure from the mule train of Nombre de Dios! You shall have a beautiful house, and magnificent clothes, and as many servants as you like, and we will live happily together, here in Plymouth. If any ill-feeling still lingers after the tragic happenings at San Juan de Ulua it will be blown away by this voyage, for we were glad to be comrades and I would have entered the gates of hell for any of my men, as they would have done for me.'

'I know it; your men have always spoken well of you. But what of Joseph—and John too, of course? How do they enjoy being rich?' Then she knew the answer to her question, for her husband's face lost its broad smile for a moment.

'Dead, as are forty of our fellow adventurers,' he said briefly. 'At Christmas time we were holed up on the coast of Darien but mighty short of food, and we had to get provisions before we could carry out the rest of our schemes. I left, with my men in one pinnace and a supporting crew in another. The *Pasha* carried too much draught to go up the rivers or into shallow harbourage. We found a ship big enough for our purpose, fully victualled and watered throughout, put the crew ashore, and turned back to our quiet anchorage, which we called Fort Diego. John had been dead a couple of days when we returned. He had been out in his ship's boat on his return and tried to capture a Spanish vessel which turned out to be fully armed. Our men had only a musket aboard! John was killed outright, as was his friend Richard Allen.'

'And Joseph?' ventured Mary timidly. 'Did Joseph die in the attack?'

'No, he died of a fever, or something like that, a few days later. I made the ship's doctor cut him open to discover how he died, for he was a good lad, Joseph. But the doctor found nothing. It must have been fever.'

Mary laid her hand on her husband's

cheek. 'You must not grieve, Frank, or feel in any way responsible for their deaths. They knew to go a-venturing with you was dangerous.' But before they could speak further on the matter they were interrupted. A slim, swarthy man said respectfully, 'Captain, I am come from Master Hawkins' house. He asked that you and your lady wife repair to Kinterbury Street without further delay.'

He bowed, and melted away into the crowd.

'A foreign looking fellow,' Drake said with a slight frown. 'How came he into the Hawkins' service?'

Mary repressed a smile. 'You *have* been long away, my love,' she said. 'I suppose you could say that Treggarron *is* a foreigner, for he comes from Cornwall, just across Tamar.'

'Hmm,' said Drake, unconvinced. 'But why should we see Hawkins now? Damn it, woman, I've not had my arms round a maid for fifteen months.' His fingers slid up her side, found the softness of her breast, and tightened. 'Damn it, I say. Hawkins can wait until we've ... spoken ... to one another.'

Mary felt the colour surge in her cheeks as her heart-beats quickened, but she said, 'Much has changed since you left England, Frank. I am sure there are things which you should know at once, and Master Hawkins knows the importance of the tidings better than I. We had better accept his invitation, my love.'

So, still holding his wife in the crook of his arm, Drake led her to the Hawkins' home, and it seemed to Mary that as they entered the parlour in Kinterbury Street, she could feel all the desire for her leave her husband, so that his mind was once again an impersonal machine that sought and found logical answers to every argument. His hand still clasped her shoulder, but it was a light touch, now, no more than a courtesy.

John Hawkins had been deep in talk with

his elder brother, William, but he broke off as they entered, and stepped forward, his hand held out. 'Drake, you've done well. Better than well, but much has happened during your absence. One thing which will concern you most nearly is the uncovering of the Ridolfi plot. It was a plot against our Queen, and Mary Stuart, may God rot her, was a party to it. The Duke of Norfolk also, though he paid for his treachery with his head.'

'Did it come to action?' Drake asked anxiously.

Hawkins, smiling, shook his head. 'No. Ridolfi was an Italian schemer and dreamer. He told the Pope, Philip of Spain and their Catholic supporters that all England would rise up against Elizabeth, if Alva would send an army into England to give aid to the Duke of Norfolk and the English Catholics. Of course it was all talk, and Cecil—who is Lord Burghley now—uncovered the whole plot with no harm done. But the Queen had been having talks with the Queen's supporters—the Scottish pretender I mean—trying to devise a way of getting the Stuart back on the throne. Seeing such treachery and underhand dealings directed against herself, who was trying to help Mary Stuart, and against her people, who wanted no part in such a plot, she despaired of ever regaining the Stuart's throne for her. Few of the Scots want Mary back, even the Bishops preach against her I'm told, and Murray, who was always against her, has been assassinated. The Scots know that Mary Stuart is all wild words and fumings against fate and even Philip and the Pope no longer trust her, or put any faith in her ability to stir up a rising in England.'

'Well, that is good, surely? Why should it affect me, though?' Drake asked, his brow furrowing.

'Well, realising that little good can come of encouraging the Stuart, Philip sees that all he is in fact doing by continuing to support the Scottish Queen, is to drive

Elizabeth—and therefore, England—into the arms of France. He has no wish for an Anglo-French alliance against Spain, you may be sure! So he is beginning to plot for a peace treaty with England, and you know that our Queen's one thought has always been to save her country from war.'

'I see. You mean that if I sailed again, I should be forced to act with friendliness towards the Spaniards who dominate the Indies?'

'More than that, Drake. There is no doubt that Spain will demand retribution against you, if it should be known that you have returned to England laden with her gold. The Queen could not say you had her warrant for your actions, for you know full well you had not, and in any case, she is trying to sue for peace so would pretend no such thing. I do not believe she would allow them to wreak their vengeance upon your life, but they would certainly demand their gold back, with the value of the ships and the booty which you captured.'

Drake nodded gloomily. 'I understand. But what can I do? I don't intend to see my men cheated out of their share of the gold they fought so hard for, neither do I intend that my backers shall be defrauded from their share.'

John Hawkins, the biggest backer, grinned approvingly. 'Well said! We have talked of this ever since news of the amity between England and Spain filtered through to us from London. If you are sensible, you'll "disappear" for a while, until it is safe for you to come into the open again. We thought, to Ireland. There you could do work for your country which would mean a great deal to the Queen, and be ready for your own work again, when this false peace ends, as it must.'

'But I'm only just home,' protested Drake, and Mary tightened her clasp on his arm. 'And Ireland will be soldiering work.'

'No, man. The Queen wants Ireland kept from Spain. The Irish are Catholics, of a sort, and there have been attempts in the past to bring her under Catholic rule from Spain. They say Spanish pirates and Scottish free-booters slink up and down the Irish seas, trying to win Ireland for themselves. It is a land of insurrection and rebellion, and Sir Walter Devereaux, who is to be made Earl of Sussex, has lately been granted a licence to endeavour to bring order and peace to Ulster. If you are willing, you can be given an introduction to him and can serve his cause, and thus win the Queen's favour.' Then, as Drake hesitated, 'Come man, it is a small choice, surely? You either lose your treasure or keep it! You can command your Spanish prize and the other frigate will also serve in the Irish campaign, under your command. We can stow your treasure away safely, in a place I know of. What will you do, eh?'

'There is no choice,' Drake said dully. 'I felt such pleasure at the thought that I was bringing England gold, which she sorely needs. But now my pleasure is as nought, for both it and the gold must be hidden. I will do as you ask.'

He accepted the Hawkins' thanks and praise for his unselfish action expressionlessly, but Mary could see that his eyes were full of veiled hurt, and his jaw was tight against the fear of expressing it. As soon as they could decently do so, they left the Hawkins's, and hurried back to Looe Street. Becky flew to the door, already full of the news that the ships were back, to find her mistress hanging on her master's arm, though neither looked happy.

'We shan't want a large dinner,' Mary said in a low voice. 'We have much to talk about. But serve the best, Becky.'

Becky flew back into the kitchen and began serving the hot food onto the dishes, whilst in the parlour Mary said as calmly as she could, 'Scarcely home, and all but chased out of my arms! You will have to go, love?' Becky came through the door, crashed the plates together, bobbed a nervous curtsey and left them to eat undisturbed. Drake, helping himself lavishly to succulent beef and piling vegetables onto his plate, nodded abstractedly.

'I suppose so. What future would there be for me if I had to answer to the Spanish like a whipped puppy? But Mary, we will arrange for the safe disposal of the treasure, and then I will see to it that a few weeks elapse before I am bound for Ireland. Lord, if I hadn't forgotten Diego!'

'Who is Diego?' asked Mary, only mildly curious.

Drake chuckled. 'He's a negro slave, who escaped from the Spaniards and guided us against them,' he explained. 'But when the time came for us to part, he did not wish to go back to the life of a hunted slave, who though he may be a leader amongst the native Indians, would be in a bad way indeed if he was ever re-captured.'

'He's here, in Plymouth?' said Mary faintly. 'But Frank, what will he do here? how will he live?'

'We had planned that he would be my servant,' Drake said ruefully. 'He is capable and very intelligent and could only be an asset to me. But as it is, I must offer him the chance of serving some other master, for he has no particular love of the sea, and would doubtless find the Irish venture miserable, for he is used to a warm, tropical climate.'

But Diego grinned a wide, white grin and declined courteously to serve another master, or to stay in the house in Looe Street to take care of his master's wife.

'My place beside you,' he said firmly. 'I don' mind the sea, do I? Gets a little sick maybe, but it be soon over. I sail with you.'

So Mary had to see her husband go again, and this time she knew when he left that his heart was full of deep and bitter disappointment. He had undertaken a perilous mission and had done well, bringing back a great treasure to swell the English coffers, and a tale of daring and courage which should gladden all English hearts. But because of the trickeries of diplomacy, he was to be cheated out of even a small measure of fame. He would have to pretend nothing had happened, that the name Nombre de Dios was just another place on the map, instead of the part of the world where he had met the Spaniards on their own ground, calmly stolen their gold from under their noses, and captured two Spanish ships to bring that same gold back to England. He could take only a secret pride in the fact that throughout all those fighting, frightening, adventurous months, he had never harmed man, woman or child. His wounds which were to him honourable scars, would now seem to have been gained in vain, and the men he had brought home alive and well could not tell the full tale of how they had gained wealth.

For Drake was determined that though he might suffer, his men who had fought and suffered with him, should never know want again. They would have a share of the treasure, enough to ensure them comfort now and the rest they would keep, as he must keep his riches, for a day when England no more had to pretend friendship with the Spaniards.

PLANS FOR A VOYAGE

'I think, Mary, that it will not be long now before your husband is back in Plymouth, able to claim his treasure.' Katherine Hawkins spoke cheerfully, aware that her young friend was beginning to think the day would never come when Drake could return to her side.

'What makes you think so, Katherine?' asked Mary. She held a needle up to the light, squinting in her efforts to thread the silk through the tiny eye.

'John has been in London, as you know. He was at court, and came home last night with some tale of the treaty for peace between England and Spain having come to an end. Apparently the agreement signed in 1573 was due for renewal this year, but nothing has come of it. The summer has already gone, and young Devereaux has sailed back to England. Soon enough your Frank will come home.'

'I wonder what he'll do then?' said Mary idly. The two women were sitting in the parlour of the house which the Hawkins used whilst in Plymouth, embroidering hangings for their London home, where they usually spent the winter months.

Mary heard a firm tread in the hall and glanced at her friend with a smile. Katherine had been married for sixteen years to her John, yet she only had to hear him approaching for her hand to go instinctively to her hair, smoothing it into place, whilst her expressive dark eyes glowed with affection. It was so now, and Mary was so busy pretending not to notice Katherine's carefully calm expression, with which she masked her inner joy, that she scarcely looked up at John Hawkins and their son Richard, as they entered the room.

Both women rose, however, and as she curtseyed, Mary saw that Richard had brought a friend in with him, for a third figure hovered in the doorway. Raising her eyes to his face, Mary gave a cry of pleasure. 'Frank!' She dropped her work on the floor and ran to her husband's arms. Turning her head against his shoulder she said accusingly, 'You knew he was coming, Katherine. You must have known!'

'No indeed,' protested Katherine, laughing. 'But John told me last night that the Earl of Essex was back in England and I thought Frank would not be far behind him. How did you fare, Frank?'

'Well enough,' said Drake, grimacing slightly. 'But I have little love for the Irish, or their seas. It is high time I came home, is it not, little one?'

'High time indeed, but Becky will have a simple supper waiting, for we did not know ... did not guess ...'

'She saw me an hour back, when my ship docked at Sutton Pool,' said Drake teasingly. 'I brought her some meat in case you were short and she is roasting and stewing a savoury repast for us both.'

Mary stifled the pang of jealousy that Becky had seen him before she had, that he had not come rushing straight to her side when his ship entered the harbour. But it was no moment for complaint. It was enough that he was here, holding her in his arms, talking of the meal they would share, the first for several months.

'So tonight I shall sleep at home, but tomorrow I must be on my way to London.'

The words brought her back to reality so sharply that his arms were no longer a safe harbour for her, but an empty promise of his warmth and companionship. 'What do you mean, Frank? You'll not leave me so soon?'

'Mary my love, I must. I have an introduction to Sir Francis Walsingham, who is a man friendly to adventures and adventurers. Others have spoken of my desire to explore and profit by those Southern seas which I saw from the coast of Darien. Richard Grenville would be before me, if he could. I need backing, and preferment. I can only get these things in London; probably only at court.' He swung her gently in his arms, as though rocking a child. 'Mary, understand me! This is for both of us, for our future. I have planned and schemed these two years, and I must grasp the opportunity of betterment with both hands, or go unsatisfied to my grave.'

'Then why should I not come with you?' Mary cried. 'Katherine goes with John when he moves to London. Why should not Becky and I pack our belongings and move to London as well?'

'An excellent idea,' broke in Hawkins as Drake hesitated. 'Believe me, Frank, you think you will move these matters in a few weeks. I tell you it will take months, perhaps a year. You had best move yourself and your household to London, find decent lodgings, and make yourself as comfortable as can be. Besides, many of the men you will meet have wives and you will no doubt want to entertain them. Do so, with your wife as hostess.'

'Say yes, Frank,' begged Mary. 'I won't hold you back or get in your way, and it would be entertaining to be in London for a while.'

'I had planned to leave tomorrow,' Drake said doubtfully. 'I was hot with impatience to get my introduction to Walsingham acted upon. Doughty, who has been a good friend to me, rides also.'

'Come, man,' said Hawkins with great good humour. 'Your gold has not yet been brought into Plymouth! Don't forget the rewards of Nombre de Dios! Surely you'll want to see the unloading of that particular cargo in person, or are you content to leave it to another?'

'No, you're right,' Drake admitted. 'I

am too impatient, as always. Yet I had thought these years had taught me patience, if nothing else. But I see you are right. I must supervise the unloading and stowage of the gold, and of course it has to be distributed to my backers, and some is still owing to the crew. It will take time, Mary. I was too hasty. We'll set out together, in a couple of weeks.'

The next few days were busy ones for Mary. She and Becky stripped the house of all the personal possessions they would need in London, and all the things most dear to them. But the majority of the hangings and all the furniture, they left.

'For dear Frank says we must buy new for London,' Mary told Becky happily as they folded linen into chests and sprinkled dried lavender among their clothes to keep them sweet. 'I wonder where we shall lodge? Some quiet street, I hope, and not too far from the Hawkins's.'

A month later, they were installed in Mary's quiet street. Frank had found them a small house which seemed suitable, jammed though it was between two much larger houses on either side. It had curly tiles on the roof and was built of grey stone and although the street was quiet enough it still had sturdy wooden shutters at the lower and upper windows. The garden was wild and needed attention, and Mary was happy to think that here, also, she would be able to enjoy making the garden, as she had done in Plymouth.

They had thought at first that a house with a garden running down to the Thames would be ideal, but such houses were costly, and it soon became evident that Drake would have other uses for his gold than spending it on housing. 'I am to visit Walsingham, in his private house at Barn Elms,' Drake told Mary jubilantly. '*Now* things should start happening!'

But the longed for visit came and went. 'You would like Sir Francis,' Drake said to his wife. 'For he is a man who loves adventure and hates the Spaniard. You should have seen his eyes light up, Mary, when I spoke of the voyage to Nombre de Dios! I told him of our first attempt on the gold train, ruined by a drunkard leaping up under the nose of a government official. When I spoke of the raid into the bay of Nombre de Dios itself, where we took the town and would have taken the Treasury had I not fainted for loss of blood, his eyes fairly started from his head! He would make a good adventurer, Mary! A bold, far-seeing, cunning man. But his health and his work keep him at home, and this makes him hot on my behalf, for it is only with his help that I shall obtain the Queen's consent for a further voyage. And this it seems I must have; even Walsingham cannot help me without the consent of her Majesty.'

'Why should the Queen give her consent to a voyage when you don't know what you may do or not do, or where you may go even, until you are there?' asked Mary practically. 'I shall want more rushes and strewing herbs in here, Frank. In winter one needs a well covered floor.'

'I may not know exactly where our voyage will lead us, but I know I shall do my best to get Spanish gold, and shall capture Spanish shipping when I need it, and trespass upon the dominions which the Spaniards regard as their own,' said Drake with a grin. 'And I need backers. The gold of Nombre de Dios will help to provide my own share, but I still need people of wealth and influence to buy shares in the venture. And of course, no one with wealth or influence can afford to displease the Queen.'

'And no one wishing to attain wealth or influence either,' said Mary acutely, and earned an approving chuckle from Drake.

'Yes, you're right. If I want wealth and influence—which I do, you minx—I must begin to conform.' He sighed reflectively. 'Outwardly, at any rate,' he concluded.

Spring came, and still Drake was closeted for hours with Walsingham. He was hopeful of seeing the Queen but a little nervous that Lord Burghley, the Queen's brilliant treasurer, would begin to wonder what an unknown young seaman was doing about the court.

'Burghley hates war, wishes for peace with Spain, and would have me stopped if he knew of my plans,' Drake told Mary gloomily. 'Mind you, I met Doughty coming from Burghley's apartments in the palace last time I was at court and he said the treasurer had offered him a secretaryship. That would have been useful to us, but Doughty turned it down. He said he didn't fancy having to work with William Cecil when behind his back he was hand in glove with me.' He sighed again. 'He's a man of honour, Thomas Doughty.'

Mary did not answer. She had been surprised to find her husband actually appearing to revere and honour this Thomas Doughty, spending long hours talking with him and quoting him frequently. It was not like Frank, who thought no man his superior, except in rank. For her own part, she found the more she saw of Thomas Doughty, the less she liked him. The man her husband called his best friend was the type of man for whom she could find no affection and little liking. He was quick witted, to be sure, and had an ingratiating way with men and women alike but Mary thought him sly and conceited, aping the manners of his betters, talking with long words where short ones would have done equally well. Still, he was her husband's friend, and as such she had to pretend complacence at any rate, when he visited the house, as he did often.

'Are you dining at home today?' she asked presently, taking down a short cloak from its hook and slipping her feet into pattens. 'I am going to try to get the garden straight, having spent so much time in the house. Spring is here, and there are daffodils choked with weeds out there, and crocuses and snowdrops already in bloom.'

Drake laughed at the wistfulness in her voice. 'You run out into your garden. It will do you good to get some fresh air into your lungs. I am going to the court again, and if all things are favourable, I may not return from there until the early hours of the morning. Sir Francis Walsingham is hopeful that the Queen's mood is such that she will see me willingly.'

'I'm glad for you, if it is so,' said Mary cheerfully, with her weeding basket on her arm, ready to go into the fresh air. 'But why should today be a better day than yesterday or tomorrow?'

Drake sighed. 'Put your basket down, for you need to concentrate hard when I talk of politics,' he said, then, relenting, 'I'll come into the garden with you. I might even pull up a few of those weeds.'

'You're more likely to pull my bulbs out,' said Mary ungratefully, but she was glad of his company and her smile was wide and sunny. They went into the garden and Mary knelt down by a weed choked border. The damp grass brushed her skirt, reminding her that she had not brought a kneeler out with her, but Drake was talking and she did not intend to disturb his train of thought with such a small matter.

'The Spaniard who has been attempting to govern the Netherlands, Alva, retired some while ago and now his replacement is leaving also. The new Governor is to be Don John of Austria, who is Philip's illegitimate brother.'

'Don John! Ah, I know of *him*. Hero of Lepanto,' said Mary with satisfaction. She so rarely knew any of the important names her husband spoke of so easily that it made her glad to be able to air her small knowledge now.

'Hmm,' grunted Drake. 'I suppose you could call him that. But he fought against the infidel Turks five years ago, when he was only twenty-four. Now the fellow hopes to prove himself not only in the Netherlands, but in England also.'

213

'Not by conquest, surely?' said Mary, fascinated. She sat back on her heels and squinted up at Drake's face as he stood with the spring sunshine behind him. 'No, I know! Marriage! I suppose he will offer himself as a suitor to the Queen, for all she's forty-two. Well, he's a real man, from the sound of it, and not really a Spaniard. She could do worse.'

'As to marriage, yes, your guess was right. But the rest is just your fancy. Now I'll leave you to think about it,' said Drake provokingly.

'Frank,' Mary wailed, 'How can I be right about marriage but wrong about the rest? Marriage with whom? There is no other of interest to us in this island! Come on, tell me what you know.'

Drake laughed and relented. 'Well, then. They say your hero of Lepanto is planning to marry Mary Queen of Scots, and then together they will seize the English throne. Now that is of interest, surely?'

'Yes; yes, I do understand,' murmured

Mary. 'The Queen knows of it, obviously. She is furious, as any English man or woman must be. And you, my dear Frank, could furnish her with the most delightful revenge. Am I right?'

'It is to be hoped you're right,' Drake said. 'So Walsingham thinks at any rate, and he's a shrewd man. I am to be presented to the Queen tonight, if she is in the right sort of mood, and then it is up to me to persuade her that our best course is to head for the Southern sea, and show the Spaniards that the Queen of England is not to be treated lightly.'

Presently he went off, humming beneath his breath, and Mary was left to her gardening and her thoughts.

She was glad, of course, that her husband would have his heart's desire; she would have been a poor wife had she wished otherwise. But she thought guiltily that she had known so little of him! Six and a half years married, and he had spent only a few months with her. She dug her gardening fork into the hard, neglected soil almost vengefully. Was it so much to ask, that he should spend a few months with her?

When Drake returned home in the early hours of the following morning, she was woken by the light falling onto her face as he pulled back the bedcurtains, his eyes shining with pride and excitement. 'I've seen the Queen, and her Grace was pleased to be charming to me, and to assure me that my voyage was just what she most desired,' he told Mary triumphantly. 'Tomorrow perhaps we will see which ships I am to be granted, how they will be fitted out, and who will come with me.'

'Tomorrow?' said Mary sleepily. 'Why tomorrow?'

Drake, wrestling with the lacings of his doublet, grunted. 'Why not?' he said. 'We've plenty of work before us, Mary. It's never too early to start work.'

'When do you hope to sail, then?' asked Mary fearfully. His reply calmed her fears, however.

'Goodness, not for months, woman! There is so much to do, and even the Queen's consent is only the beginning. Furthermore, all our preparations must be done in the utmost secrecy, which will naturally take longer. Come now, be glad that our voyage is set, but don't fear that I shall be leaving you too soon. Preparations for a voyage of this kind take time.'

★ ★ ★ ★

For the best part of the year of preparation, Mary and Frank were in London. Mary tended her garden, talked with the wives of men who wished to take part in the expedition, entertained for her husband, and saw the sights of London. She and Becky gazed open-mouthed at the Tower of London, but derived more pleasure from the beasts in the menagerie than from the great fortress. They shopped in the Royal Exchange, buying, for the first time in their lives, the best of everything, although they did not spend with abandon, because Drake thought always of the fitting out of his fleet first and foremost. But Mary gained considerable pleasure from going with her husband on shopping expeditions for the furnishings of his cabin. They bought fine silverware, serving dishes, goblets for the wine, snowy white damask for tablecloths and napkins; even kitchen utensils. But most carefully of all were chosen a stock of the best drawing paper and water colours, inks and quill pens. For Drake was an artist of no mean order, and whenever his duties permitted, he would chart the coasts along which he had sailed, and illustrate the charts with pictures of the landfalls he made.

Several of the men who would sail with her husband became good friends; they met in Drake's London lodgings to talk anxiously of John Oxenham's small expedition, which had set out hastily and with little or no preparation to try to forestall Drake in his attempt to get through the Straits of Magellan into that Spanish dominated Southern sea. He had been with Drake on the mainland when the Cimarroons had bidden them climb the great tree, from whose branches a view could be obtained of that sea where no English ship had ever sailed, and he had heard Drake vow to venture into that sea. 'I will be with you, or if not, I'll go before you!' he had declared, and though Drake said that Oxenham had not sufficiently prepared himself or his vessels, Mary knew that he worried in case his friend really did become the first Englishman to conquer the Straits.

But in truth, he had not much time to spare to worry over Oxenham's expedition. He seemed to be everywhere at once, planning with this one, scheming with that one. One minute he would be sky-high with exhilaration, then sunk in the depth of despair as the political climate changed and it seemed certain they would never sail.

At last, however, their plans seemed definite enough for them to move back to Plymouth and it was with only a small pang of regret that Mary began to pack up her goods and chattels to return to her home town. And when they arrived in Looe Street once more, Plymouth seemed sweet to them both after the noise and heat of London. The fresh tang of the sea greeted their nostrils when they awoke in the morning, instead of the smell which rose out of the Thames in early summer, and was strong enough to turn even a Londoner's stomach. The noise of the gulls overhead and the calling of the people in the streets seemed like sweet music after the continual clatter and loud, constant ware-calling of the big city.

Mary visited Annie, and saw her sister with her family around her, proud mother now of three sons and two daughters. No one commented on Mary's childless state, however, and for this she was thankful. Mary knew that Frank, like every other man of her acquaintance, would have liked sons to carry on his family name. But he seemed resigned now to the fact that she was not going to become pregnant. During the earlier years of their marriage, he had always asked after the state of her health, hoping that she would be able to tell him that she, too, was going to bear a child. Now, after a year at home with her, he seemed to have given up all thoughts of a family and concentrated instead on his beloved ships.

Mary was aware that the first bloom of their love had faded, but she made no effort to try to arouse her husband's interest. He is wedded to the sea, she thought. It would only make him feel guilty and wretched if he knew that sometimes I feel lonely and neglected. So she went about her work in the house, tended her garden, and began to take an interest in the affairs of the town. She visited the poor, and gave employment when she could to the women whose babies would never know their father, and who might otherwise have been driven from the town. She talked to the men with whom her husband would spend the next year or so: the Doughty brothers, Thomas, who had served with Drake in Ireland and who amused Mary by his preoccupation with the clothing he should take on the voyage, and his younger brother, John. Closer association with the Doughty brothers had not lessened her first, instinctive aversion to Thomas, and she liked John even less.

'John Doughty was thrown into prison, and laid there a year, for poisoning the Earl of Essex,' she said righteously to Annie. 'Can you wonder that I do not like him?'

'He's a personable young man, though,' Annie said, 'And surely you don't believe that he poisoned any Earl? Why, whatever would the likes of him be doing poisoning the nobility?'

Mary laughed unwillingly. 'Well, perhaps it was said that he'd been instrumental in poisoning the Earl,' she admitted. 'Anyway, I don't like him or his brother.'

'Mary, you've listened to enough gossip in your time to be able to sort out the facts of the case,' Annie said reprovingly. 'From what I've heard, the poor young fellow probably gave tongue to the suspicion held by a number of people; that Leicester had poisoned Essex so that he could have the Earl's wife.'

'Maybe so,' Mary agreed, 'but there seems to be trouble wherever the Doughtys go. Frank did not hear of it at the time, but when he and Tom Doughty were in Ireland, the Earl of Essex sent Doughty with a message to the court, to try to find out whether someone there was working against him. I'm not sure of the ins and outs of the affair, but Ireland breeds insecurity in Englishmen, they say. Anyhow, when Doughty returned from England, he told Essex that Leicester was his enemy, whispering in the Queen's ear to his detriment. The Earl of Essex determined to have the matter out with the Earl of Leicester, and then he discovered that Doughty had filled him full of lies, to set Devereaux and Leicester at loggerheads. Why, there was quite a to do over it at the time, I believe, with Lord Burghley acting as peacemaker.'

'Yes, the fellow's a mischief-maker, that's plain enough,' acknowledged Annie. 'But maybe it is only because he lacks occupation and makes trouble from boredom. Surely on this voyage, he'll be too busy to do anything but sleep when his work is done?' Mary looked unconvinced, but did not argue the matter further.

Others who would sail with Drake won her warmest admiration: John Chester, a small, thin man with a lean, intelligent face carved into deep furrows when he smiled. William Hawkins, a cheerful lad completely at home in a ship, who had been apprenticed to the sea from an early age and who was almost as easy with Mary as with his cousin, Richard

Hawkins. John Wynter she knew to be a fine sailor, though he was not at his ease with women and yet another John, John Thomas, she also found pleasant company. At first he had been regarded with some suspicion because of clerkly inclinations and also because Christopher Hatton, a great favourite of the Queen and one of the biggest backers of the expedition, had insisted that Thomas command a vessel. But soon all liked him for himself.

Tom Moone, who had sailed on the Nombre de Dios voyage as carpenter in the *Swan*, was an old friend. Mary liked the bluff and cheerful seaman, who had made her laugh with his tales of the first voyage, especially the piece of chicanery which had sunk the *Swan* and, he used to say, won him a command in this exploit.

'For the *Swan* was an impediment in Drake's plan to use the pinnaces for most of the inshore and attacking work,' he explained to Mary. 'As long as he had two ships, he must always leave sufficient men to sail both, whilst he undertook the attacks on towns and shipping with a force too small for success. So he decided that the *Swan* must be scuttled, which would release more men for the pinnaces. But his brother captained her, and he was mortal fond of John. So he sent for me, and told me to bore three holes through her bottom as near to the keel as might be, and then cover them carefully so that none might see how the water was entering. I did it, in mortal dread of being caught and having my throat cut! Men grow fond of a ship that has served them well, see? Even the Admiral knew he would have his work cut out to persuade the men who sailed in the *Swan*, his brother and all, that it was to their advantage to scuttle her.

'Next morning, your husband came alongside in a little rowboat and invited his brother to go fishing. My, the fishing was good in those waters! You only had to cast your line and the fish were fighting for the privilege of being pulled aboard! But

Cap'n John was busy, and said he would join Drake later. As your husband pulled away, he called out casually as if he had in truth just that moment noticed, "Why is your ship so low in the water?" And when they went to investigate, the water below decks was waist deep. Everyone was surprised, because not a drop of water had she taken before; the *Swan* was in truth a good ship. So we manned the pumps. My, how we worked!' He chuckled at the recollection. 'And I had to work as hard as any, and catching the Admiral's eye I had hard ado not to smile, for he was working grimly, as though he was determined to save the vessel.

'By three in the afternoon we could see it was hopeless, and the Admiral, milady, graciously told John he would stand down as captain of the *Pasha* so that John could take his place. The Admiral said he would command naught but his pinnace, the *Minion,* until such time as we had captured ourselves another vessel. The

Swan was burnt when she was empty of the men and their gear, so that she could not fall into Spanish hands.'

'I've often wondered why the Admiral chose to call his pinnace the *Minion*,' Mary said thoughtfully. 'After all, the *Minion* was the ship in which John Hawkins and the survivors escaped from San Juan de Ulua. I should not have thought the name could have had happy memories for my husband.'

Tom Moone coughed respectfully. 'I've wondered also, milady. Maybe he named his pinnace thus because the *Minion* survived the horrors of de Ulua and he feels it to be a lucky name; or maybe he used it to remind himself that lives come before gold or fame. Certainly he never forgets it.'

'One day I may ask him,' said Mary, smiling. 'But I admit I have not done so yet.'

But one factor made it difficult for Mary to be entirely at ease with these men. Only a handful of them knew their destination, and Mary was not sure whether they really knew that the voyage was one of deliberate annoyance to Spain. But the youngest boy who would ship aboard the *Pelican,* Drake's flagship, was yet another John, Drake's fourteen-year-old cousin. He was a delightful lad with smooth blond hair falling over his tanned forehead, and a pair of wide, innocent blue eyes. Mary knew that Thomas, her husband's youngest brother, was in the secret but she did not find her brother-in-law a particularly congenial person. He was aggressive and self-assured, patronising Mary before their friends and always trying to keep his adored elder brother's attention directed towards himself. But Johnny Drake was different; eager, willing, and a good listener. He and Mary enjoyed many a thrilling guessing game of the adventures which lay ahead of them, and though Johnny knew almost as much about their intentions as did the most important of the backers, he kept his secret knowledge close.

Once again, of the ordinary seamen not a man was pressed; they had flocked to join Drake of their own accord. They were willing to sail to an unknown destination under a seaman who had not yet won himself a famous name because they had heard of his skills and humanity from those others, who had sailed with him to Nombre de Dios. 'The Admiral will see us right,' was their comfortable philosophy, and Mary was proud to share their belief.

The gentlemen who wished to sail to gain a fortune soon realised that their leader was no ordinary mariner, but a man with tremendous force of character and abounding energy combined with a talent for navigation and seamanship which he had nurtured and expanded until the talent had swelled into a genius.

When Autumn came and the ships were fitted out and snug, England began to be busy indeed; the Netherlands had risen in revolt against their hated Spanish overlords many times, but though Elizabeth had helped them with money and advice, she had refused to become embroiled in a war. Then, with the ending of the French civil war, the Duke of Guise offered to join the Governor of the Province, Don John of Austria, to crush the Protestant states. Englishmen began to flock to the continent as volunteers to aid the Netherlands, and by the time Drake was ready to sail, war fever was at its height.

So that on 15th November, Mary and the relatives of others of the crews of the *Pelican*, the *Elizabeth*, the *Marigold*, the *Swan* and the *Benedict*, waved to their men, whilst the rest of England kept their eyes firmly fixed on the Narrow Seas. The proposed voyage to annoy the Spaniard had begun, and no one had even noticed!

11

NO OTHER LOVE

'So you are convinced that Frank is dead, Jan? Well, you must be, as you've asked me to marry you.' Mary twisted round to face her companion, but he was not looking at her. He was examining his fingernails with every appearance of rapt attention and when he spoke, he still did not meet her eyes.

'Everyone believes he is dead, except you. Consider the facts, Mary! Captain Wynter confirmed that three of the ships got safely through the Magellan Straits, including his own *Elizabeth* and the craft your husband sailed in. But he also told you that they met foul weather almost immediately and after the most dreadful trials, were separated. He told you how he searched, and waited, and finally decided that Drake and his crew must have been drowned in the tremendous gales; then he sailed for England once more, having no stomach for a solitary expedition. Since then—nothing. No word has reached you, none of the ships have returned. Surely it is time that you considered marrying again, if only for companionship?'

Mary lay back on the grass and gazed up into the leafy sun-dazzle of the chestnut tree above her. They were in a little wood, on the outskirts of Dartmoor, taking advantage of the lovely summer day. Their horses cropped the grass nearby, hobbled so that they could not canter off to their wild moorland cousins, and the two young people savoured the freedom of the open country where they could be alone.

'I'll not pretend to marry you for companionship. If I should marry you, it will be for love,' Mary said firmly but with wildly beating heart. 'Yet Jan, you have a certain reputation with women, but towards me you have shown only gentle understanding and affection. Now you suddenly offer me marriage, a home—and your love. Surely it is natural enough that I am surprised that you should be willing to give up your freedom?'

Jan was quiet for a moment, considering her. Sometimes, he thought, he surprised himself. Why indeed, did he wish to marry this small, pale girl, with her skin like milk and her slender figure? He liked his women to be bold and colourful, with easy manners to match their rounded generous bodies. At twenty-eight he'd had no thought of marrying unless for obvious economic reasons. Yet Mary was no rich widow—one of the reasons as yet unspoken for his sudden decision to ask her to become his wife was the shrewd suspicion that the money Drake had left was beginning to run out.

I've never even kissed her, he thought suddenly. The conventional kiss of greeting between friends perhaps, but nothing more. He had felt desire for her, of course, but had satisfied his lust with the easy women who thronged the port of Plymouth though he felt guilty because it was possible for him to satisfy the hunger Mary roused in him, and so impossible for her.

'Why do you wish for marriage, Jan?' Mary asked again.

Suddenly, the answer was so strong and urgent that it burned within him, a fire of lust which only she could quench. What did he want with the whores of the waterfront? They had none of the freshness of true love, which this slim, light haired girl had in such abundance. They could quiet his appetites, but never satisfy him as he knew in his heart Mary could. He seized her shoulders and pushed her against the trunk of the chestnut tree, bringing his mouth down on hers so abruptly that their noses banged and Mary sqeaked as the water came stinging to her eyes. Wriggling, she broke free for an instant and pushed against Jan's broad chest whilst he grappled with her, all the long months of careful coolness towards a married woman forgotten now that he had held her in his arms.

But he had no desire to force her, and loosed her sulkily, hurt by her apparent revulsion at his embrace. Mary smiled up at him teasingly. 'There's a root poking me in the back,' she explained breathlessly, in a voice which shook a little. 'You would not have me kiss you with half my mind intent on my shoulder blade? Let us lie on my cloak.'

Calmly, she reached for the soft folds of velvet and spread the garment out on the grass. Then she glanced at him, her eyes half shy, half inviting and he fell upon her, his lips meeting her mouth this time with no awkwardness. He barely had time to notice that this time her body moved to meet him, that her touch was tender yet as eager as his own, before the wave of his pleasure broke over him so that he was deaf to birdsong and blind to sunlight, living only for that triumphant moment of love.

* * * *

So it was to be marriage with Jan for her, after all. As she prepared for bed in the room she and Frank had shared together, Mary thought that after her abandoned behaviour that afternoon, it was natural enough that Jan should expect it. Yet she had given him no definite answer, and still wondered uneasily what she should do. For though Frank had been gone so long that to think of him was not, now, a bright stab of anguish twisting in her breast, yet she still found it impossible to imagine a world without him, devoid of that restless, courageous, self-confident presence. And if she could not believe she was a widow, then she would be doing wrong both to Jan and to Frank to re-marry.

In her bed, she tried to turn her thoughts

from her problem to the more mundane though no less pressing one of planning her winter larder; for with so little money, the planning would have to be good, allowing for no waste of any description. But she could not drag her thoughts away from the two men. Strangers, she thought, would have found them very different but in many ways they were alike. Perhaps in a way, she loved Jan the more because he reminded her of Frank. Both were men of courage and imagination, men who were not afraid of the unknown, who found adventure a challenge. It had been her misfortune, perhaps, that Frank's courage and imagination had taken him away from her, so that when he was in her company he still thought longingly of the wonders he might have been exploring. Jan, on the other hand, had been soldiering in Ireland and on the continent, had sailed the seas in quest for gold or trade, yet when he was with her, Mary knew that she was his main preoccupation. For him, his small estate whose meadows dropped down to the sea so that he made a dual harvest, silver loads of fish from the water and gold grain from his fields, was as much a challenge as the promise of war with Spain or France. And his relationship with his wife would be a challenge also, she was sure, and not merely something which he took for granted.

She turned restlessly between the sheets, crushing a spray of lavender between her fingers so that the scent rose, warm and vibrant, to caress her nostrils in the velvet dark. Why should she not marry Jan? They loved one another, and she had found a dizzying, singing pleasure in his arms that afternoon which she had never achieved with Frank. She remembered the nights she had spent in this very bed with her husband, and in retrospect it seemed sometimes that only their mutual desire for a child had led to lovemaking. She thought crossly that even if he came whistling home from across the world, with a fortune in his pocket, he would merely give her a quick and careless kiss before going off again. Perhaps he would go to court to see the Queen, or to France to see a friend. But he would go away from her. He would scarcely notice her once the first novelty of reunion was over.

But suppose he came home, to find her married to Jan? She tried to shrug the thought away, reminding herself of the many little inattentions, the increasing indifference to his wife that the years had brought. But she had not grown so far apart from Frank in almost three years that she could not wince at his hurt. He might not be demonstrative, he might be neglectful even, but she was not deceived into believing that he did not love her. His grief would be deep and sincere, and would ruin for him the success—if any—that his voyage had achieved.

Resolutely, she turned over in bed and switched her mind to the contents of her store cupboard. If she could find someone to smoke a quantity of pork for her, since she had no facilities for doing it in Looe Street ...

* * * *

With a lover's ardour, Jan was knocking on the front door before Mary had finished her breakfast, but since she had not yet confided in Becky she merely smiled at him and asked him to wait whilst she put on her taffeta cloak. Then they went down to the town together, for Jan wished to make a purchase in the market.

'Are you searching for bargains amongst the dairy produce and the fruit stalls?' Mary asked teasingly.

'My housekeeper would draw and quarter me! No, Mary, I would like to buy you a ring. Not a good one here, of course, just a trinket. But something for you to wear for me until I buy you a better, when I take you to London as my wife.'

'But we are not *betrothed*,' Mary said

uncomfortably. 'It is too bad of me Jan, to refuse to give you an answer, but I cannot feel sure in my own mind that Frank is really dead. I've prayed to God for guidance, for some sign that I am a widow or not, but today with the sun high in the heavens and my best gown on, I cannot be sure of anything save that I am happy.'

'If you get no sign within three days, we shall marry,' Jan said as sternly as he could, but the pleasure bubbled out of him in laughter, because he was so sure of Mary, now. She laughed with him, pressing close to him in the good natured market throng.

It was a happy morning. They squabbled affectionately over the choice of a ring, both loudly decrying the other's taste in gemstones, and then both deciding on the same small blue stone with its ring of diamond chips, their eyes speaking of love as he put the circle on her finger, though their lips only smiled.

They did not have a meal at mid-day, but shared a bag of oatmeal biscuits and strong local cheese, followed by fruit. 'We could have had a dinner at the tavern, but it is so pleasant in the sunshine,' Jan told her, and she agreed with him as they strolled up to the Hoe and watched a crowd of children playing tag.

It was whilst they were on the Hoe that they noticed the crowd far below them, around the edge of Sutton Pool.

'The fishermen have had a good catch,' speculated Jan, but Mary thought not.

'It's that boat—the one with the Frenchy look about her rigging—that is drawing the people down to the quay,' she said. 'I wonder, Jan—can it be news from foreign parts? There *is* a crowd! Do let's go and see what is happening.'

They sauntered down to the quayside, in no hurry, but were disappointed when they arrived to find that the crowd was dispersing.

'Please—what has been happening here?'

243

asked Mary, seizing a loiterer by the sleeve. 'We saw the crowd—what news has been brought?'

The man was eager to tell his tale to someone still in ignorance. 'They brought news of a Spanish wickedness,' he said. 'A Devonshire adventurer, a man of Plymouth in fact, has been captured and hung in the square at Lima by those devils of the Inquisition. All because of their spite against us protestants, they cut down the flower of our manhood whenever they can catch them.'

Mary stood quite still, feeling the blood drain from her face as she saw the scene in her mind. The dusty square, thick with people come to watch the Englishman die, the white-hot glare and dazzle from the buildings and the tired droop of palms against the sky of tropical blue. She imagined the cruel complacency of the brown peasant faces as the figure clad in yellow to show his faith came out amongst them to kick and choke and die on the gallows, like a common felon.

The pleasant picture of Sutton Pool swam unsteadily before Mary's eyes, but she forced herself into a semblance of calmness. 'His name, sir? For pity's sake, was the man's name Drake?'

'Aye, milady, that'll be the man. Or was it Oxenham they hanged, and Drake who is still a prisoner?' mused the man thoughtfully. 'Well no matter, for both were good Devonshire men. And this first one was hung many, many months ago so whichever 'twas, the other may have followed him by now.'

Mary saw the seamed face before her tilt and blur, and was aware of a cool rushing sensation against her cheeks, then the cobbles swung lazily into her face and exploded in a rash of coloured stars. Darkness clouded her brain, and she knew no more.

She recovered consciousness to find herself lying on the couch in her own parlour, with Becky leaning over her and

Jan crouching on the floor near her head, holding her limp hand.

'I'm sorry,' she said faintly. 'But the shock ... he was speaking of Frank, was he not, Jan?'

'Perhaps. Or maybe of John Oxenham,' Jan said as gently as he could. 'It is small comfort I realise, my love, but at least this should answer your question. I think there can be little doubt that you are a widow, and therefore free to marry again.'

Becky shot a startled look at her mistress, then at the young man who gazed at her lady with such troubled love. She was not surprised that it had come to talk of marriage, for she had read love in Master Jan's eyes for many a month, but she was somehow surprised that her mistress had agreed to it. Not that Master Jan wasn't a proper man, and one who'd make any woman glad to bed with him, she added hastily to herself. But Master Frank now, he was one in a million, and though not perhaps the most understanding and affectionate of husbands, she had always believed her mistress valued him too highly to take another. From what she'd gathered, someone had spoken of his death, which ought to allow her lady to take another man for her husband, and no question. Yet the surprise still lingered.

Mary caught the maid's glance, and said apologetically, 'I'm sorry, Becky. I had meant to tell you myself that Master Jan had offered me marriage. I had not accepted him, believing that my husband still lived, but now ...' she sighed, and rubbed her brow like a fretful child. 'I suppose I have to believe myself widowed, now,' she concluded.

As soon as Mary felt sufficiently strong, Becky and Jan helped her to her bed-chamber. Jan left, with a promise to call round early the next morning to see how she fared, and Becky got her mistress between the sheets and made her a poppied draught so that she could sleep—for one glance at that white, distraught face was enough to convince the maid that normal sleep would not visit her mistress that night.

So Mary slept—but this was no health restoring slumber but a plague of nightmares which had her whimpering into her pillow and throwing off the bedclothes as she tossed and turned, trying to find peace from her dreadful imaginings.

The square at Lima blazed, with the dead man on the gallows at one moment wearing Frank's face, the next, Jan's. She fled from it, to be pursued by the great crosses of the Inquisition carried by sinister, black robed monks. She jumped into the sea to swim to England, and the water turned to honey, sucking her down. She could not swim in it—but great sharks could, nosing against her as they decided where and when to snap.

Suddenly, she was pulled swiftly and smoothly from the nightmare brightness of Lima to quite a different scene. She was looking down from the sky upon a ship, as it lay motionless in the water. Or at least, that was her first impression. Then she realised that in fact, the vessel was stranded on a great whale-backed ridge of rock, over which the waves broke and pounded. Her sides were encrusted with barnacles and seaweed, and the men on her decks wore silks and satins in the Spanish fashion, yet she saw Frank striding about issuing orders and knew she was looking down at his ship and his crew, cast upon a rock somewhere on the wide ocean, with no sight of land.

The activity on deck began to have a meaning for her. They were lightening the cargo, that was what they were doing! The cannon from the deck went first, crashing into the sea so that the water seemed to boil. Others followed, and then sacks of grain, peas, beans—her heart bled for the precious supplies which were being jettisoned. Then the men lugged up from below a quantity of spice of some sort, which coloured and perfumed the salt sea for one moment so that Mary thought 'Cloves!' and knew that the situation must be every bit as desperate as it looked, for spices were worth their weight in gold to Englishmen.

A little later she realised that the tide was being closely watched from the decks of the small ship, and saw two lads lowered into the water to take a look at the hull.

Presently she grew interested in the position of the ship. She was wedged, apparently immovably, on a ledge of rock, with the sea on one side of her so deep that it looked an intense inky black, yet so clear that she could see the rock going down, down, and still down, a mighty undersea mountain. And the other side of the ship was washed by barely a foot of the clear, pale green water, which lapped round her planking almost lovingly whilst shoals of tiny, vivid fish darted inquisitively around this monster which had suddenly appeared in their midst.

Even as she watched, the men knelt in

prayer, and as though in cruel answer, the wind blew a strong gust which caught the vessel amidships. She started to heel over, and even as the men cried out in alarm and began crowding to the other side of the ship to try to counteract the tilt, the wind caught her again and the sails swung over. Almost before Mary had realised what was happening, the cruel rocks which had gripped the keel of the vessel in their teeth gave up their prey, and the ship slid off the ledge and bounded on the depths of the ocean out of danger once more, bobbing like a cork in the swell from the reef.

Some trick of the dream prevented Mary hearing anything said on board the vessel, though she could hear the suck and gurgle of the waves on the reef, the flap of the sail and the wind singing in the rigging. But she did not need to be able to hear when her own heart, too, was filled with the joy of the deliverance which was singing in the hearts of every man aboard the vessel below her, as the captain obviously gave a volley of orders which sent his men scurrying to trim the sails and set all to rights. She watched, in a daze of gladness, as the ship took the wind eagerly into her sails and began to move with increasing sureness away from the shoalwater. Soon, she was a small thing, a toy, heading for the distant horizon, her wake straight as a ruler laid across the surface of the ocean to prove how steady was the hand which steered her course.

Mary awoke, to find the tears of fear and joy still wet on her cheeks, whilst for the first time in many months she knew the comfort of a quiet mind. There could be no doubt—there *was* no doubt—that this was the sign for which she had prayed. The other had been false. She was sorry for John Oxenham (for she was sure now, that he had died on the gallows in Lima) but her joy in the knowledge of Frank's safety outweighed all else.

As she dressed, she thought a trifle ruefully, that it would not be easy to

252

convince Jan that she was most certainly not a widow, that in a few weeks time perhaps, her husband would be sailing his ship into Sutton Pool. She even recognised that once the first elation of her uncannily realistic dream wore off, she herself might begin to doubt. She knew, too, that her love for Jan was deep and real, as was his love for her; that it might well have been better for them both had they married, for few would deny her the right after three years of silence. But she had made a marriage vow to 'cleave only unto him, as long as we both shall live', and vows such as that were not made to be broken.

As she began to descend the stairs, she heard Becky opening the front door to Jan and knew a craven desire to creep back to her bed and feign illness. Then she stiffened her back and continued to go downstairs. She had watched Frank fight for the life of his men and his ship and never look glum or appear to have doubts. Should she show cowardice over this other matter? As she walked steadily into the parlour she reminded herself that it had only been a dream, after all. Or had it?

12

HOMECOMING

'We're home, lads! Look, you can see the chalk of the cliffs, and the town crouching at the water's edge. When we round Rame Head we'll be in the Sound, and soon enough, on dry land once more!' Drake's words were greeted with a subdued, ecstatic murmur; the murmur of men who have been long absent, when they approach their homeland across the blue of the sea.

As the *Golden Hind* rounded the point, a fisherman in his small bark gazed up at them. He could see their gaping seams, the encrusted sides of the little ship, and knew she had sailed in tropical waters. But many ships came into Plymouth Sound from outlandish voyages to strange places. The men on her decks were bearded and deeply tanned; they were well-dressed for mariners, he thought, though their once fine silks and velvets were the worse for seawater and long wear.

Then, from the deck, a voice hailed him. A warm voice, with the strength of one accustomed to command. 'Is the Queen alive?' it called.

'Very much so,' replied the fisherman, amazed that anyone—particularly an Englishman—should be in doubt on that score. Since they seemed to have voyaged long, however, he added the information that the plague was raging in Plymouth, and they would be well advised not to lower their anchor in Sutton Pool. But his caution was little heeded aboard the vessel, for a ragged cheer ran round the deck above his head, hands waved and gestured, and then the *Golden Hind* caught the wind, bobbed and curtseyed, and made for Plymouth Sound with the wind singing in her rigging almost as loudly as the mariners sang on her decks.

The fisherman scratched his head, then shrugged and returned to his task of casting out his nets. He had warned them about the plague, there was little else he could do. He watched the strange craft until it disappeared from sight behind St Nicholas Island, then turned away. He mused for a moment over the identity of the vessel; she had an outlandish name enough, and one which he certainly could not identify. Yet there was something about the cut of her, the panache with which she was sailed ... he chided himself for idle speculation when all would become clear on his return home in the evening and turned resolutely once more to his work. The strange vessel could keep, but the fish had to be caught when the weather allowed him to take his boat out of the harbour.

★ ★ ★ ★

Mary and Becky had been berrying on the Hoe, and saw the small ship sail into the Sound. With their hearts in their mouths, they abandoned their baskets of blackberries and ran helter skelter down to Sutton Pool, but no ship was yet to be seen.

'There are fishing craft out today, perhaps they warned the vessel that the pestilence is hot in the streets still, because the warm weather has lingered,' suggested Becky and Mary, nodding, ran with her skirts looped over her arm to the home of her nearest friend.

'They're back, Frank and his crew,' she gasped. 'They haven't landed, but I believe they're anchored in the Sound. Could I go out to them? Would it be permitted for someone to row me out to the ship? I am—God be thanked—free from the pestilence though I have nursed others.'

The worthy citizen hurried off, and much sooner than Mary had dared to hope, she was sitting in the bows of a rowing boat with John Blythman, the Mayor of Plymouth, and they were skimming across the waves of the Sound towards the ship which now lay at anchor in full view of the town.

She looked weary, thought Mary with compassion, taking in the caked sides and the gaping seams of her husband's craft, much as the fisherman had done earlier. But then three years of constant sailing in the tropics were enough to make any ship feel old. Then they were alongside, and eager hands were helping her onto the deck. She looked round at the faces—bearded, every one—and knew tears were running down her cheeks, tears of joy. Then Drake, the tears chasing each other into the magnificent growth of his beard embraced her quickly, and took her and the Mayor down to his cabin.

Once there, Drake pulled her onto his knee, smoothing her shining hair. 'Mary, my darling, we have much news for you, and I have many, many gifts which should gladden your heart, for they prove that I thought of you constantly,' he told her lovingly. 'Now dry your eyes, and don't cry any more, or the men will think you are sorry we have returned safely.'

Mary sniffed, and swallowed hard. 'I'm sorry to weep, my love,' she said, blowing her nose hard into an inadequate little handkerchief. 'But it's been so long, Frank ...' Her voice broke and she buried her face into his salty, stained doublet.

'I know, love. It has been a long time for us also, but we have been too busy for repining, and this has made the waiting time much easier to bear. Now John Blythman, welcome to the *Golden Hind!* I am sorry if I seem a neglectful host, but as ever, I am in a hurry. Can you tell me how England will view my return? How do I stand with the Queen? Do you have the latest news from London?'

Blythman shook his head doubtfully. 'I'm not a man of much learning,' he said, 'But some trouble you're bound to face. Wynter brought a tale back that you'd put a man of Hatton's to death for treason and witchcraft, and had taken a Portuguese prize. Of the fellow's death I can't speak, but England is friendly with Portugal now, since the Queen supports the pretender to the throne, to annoy the Spaniards who have put King Philip in power.'

'Wynter is alive? His crew also? Well, I'm heartily glad of it,' said Drake. 'As for Doughty—you knew it was Thomas Doughty that was put to death, the man who called himself my friend?—I will answer for that when I see his patron, Sir Christopher Hatton. But why should taking a Portuguese prize two years ago affect my reception now?'

Mary lifted her head from his shoulder and said, 'Frank, Wynter was afraid of being charged with desertion, so he said he'd left you because you took the Portuguese ship; he knew that would make him popular with Burghley, and some others. He believed you dead of course, so thought nothing he could say would harm you.'

'I ... see,' Drake said after a moment. 'But what of the Queen, my heart? What is her opinion of my exploits?'

'No one knows,' admitted Mary miserably. 'I didn't even realise that she would have known you lived—I did not know for certain, and I am your wife. But I didn't believe she has had much time to think about you, of late. She has been threatened by Spain; at the beginning of the month the Spaniards landed troops in Ireland to undermine the English there and to stir up more trouble in Ireland. A ... a ... friend of mine, Master Jan, sailed with the loyal troops. Some people say that if you were alive it would be to your advantage since it is from Spain that complaints will come, no doubt?' She smiled at his nod. 'I thought so! But the Queen changes her mind from one day to the next, I believe.'

'It is true that her Grace does change her mind frequently,' Drake admitted, 'But if she decides to stand a man's friend, nothing will change that. Blythman, I think the best thing I can do is send young Brewer off to London to see the Queen and my backers. I have letters written. Could you arrange a horse for him?'

Blythman agreed without demur but Mary said anxiously, 'John Brewer is only a lad, Frank. He's not much older than our dear nephew, Johnny. Is it wise to send him on an errand of such importance?'

'Our dear Johnny stands at your elbow, all six feet of him,' said her husband, as the young man entered the cabin in response to his peal on a small handbell. 'He's seventeen, Mary, and so is Brewer. Further, Brewer is a trustworthy and presentable young man, and one far better to undertake an errand of this magnitude than some reliable old seadog.'

'The years have changed everyone,' Mary said, awed. 'But to see little boys who have changed into great men—that is the biggest surprise of all.'

Johnny, blushing deeply, said, 'It is nature, cousin Mary. It would be strange indeed if at seventeen I still had a complexion like a girl, and a voice like a choirboy!'

When the boat returned to the shore with Blythman and Brewer, however, Mary did not accompany them. At her husband's request, she shared a narrow bed in the master's cabin with him, delighted that though he might not come ashore yet, she could still be with him. And even in the first ecstasy of their reunion, she noticed affectionately how gently he took his pleasure, his mind and body asking, never demanding.

After they were back on dry land once more, she thought the three days she spent on board the *Golden Hind* were some of the happiest she had ever known. They lay close, under the lee of St Nicholas Island and out of sight of the town, where the pestilence still took its daily toll.

Here Frank talked to her, as he had never somehow found time to do before.

'We sought refuge here, my parents and their family, when our Protestant religion gave offence to Henry VIII,' he told her once, indicating the island looming above them. 'Strange, my love, that St Nicholas should have given me sanctuary when I was still in petticoats, and now he does so again.'

Mary leaned on his shoulder, idly watching the bobbing waves as they lapped gently against the rocks. 'Were you here long, as a lad, Frank?'

'Not long. For we soon had to flee again, and then we went to Gillingham Reach and lived in the hull of an old ship, afloat on the Medway. Father preached to the fleet in secret, and as soon as I was old enough I was apprenticed as a fisherman, casting for cod off the dogger bank, working until I could have slept on my feet. Cold often, hungry often. But content!' he laughed. 'By God, Mary, sometimes I think only the young know true, uncomplicated happiness. There was I, a scraggy urchin, with lice in my hair and chapped hands; blisters the size of crowns all over my feet and only rags to protect me from the biting cold wind. I smelt of fish, and worse. But I sang about my work, whistled as I gutted the great cod, flapped barefoot over the cobbles with a light heart, because I had always wanted to go to sea, and it was enough for me that I had my heart's desire. But sometimes we traded, carrying goods across the channel, and that was better for comfort, though not so good for navigation. We learned the hard way how to navigate when we chased the canny codfish, who knew the sea paths better than I knew the land. And the shoals of herring, in their season, taught me many a trick. So when old Will, the master of the bark, died and left me his vessel, I had a trade at my fingertips.' He smiled at Mary's compassionate expression. 'Oh, don't feel sorry for me, my love! For I was young, and I loved the sea then as I love it now. One moment I was a lad who worked hard for his bread and the next I was the Master! By God, those were wonderful days, when I woke in the morning knowing I owned a little ship; I could choose my own way, take me a crew. I could be after the cod when fishing was good, or I could trade across the channel. The world of the sea was at my feet; in my own hands and in my ship my fortune lay. I was happy!'

'And now?' Mary murmured softly.

He smiled again, his face confident. 'Now we wait for words from the Queen. But though she has the power to keep fame and fortune from me, whilst I own a ship and have the means and strength to sail her, I cannot know much grief.'

'Tell me about your voyage round the world,' Mary begged, eager to hear about his adventures in the tropic seas, so that as he recounted stories of the strange sights and stranger happenings she too could share in the adventure, albeit at secondhand. But he said he did not want to speak of the voyage. There was too much at stake to chatter about it, when all his hopes hung in the balance.

'When the Queen gives her decision, then you'll have your work cut out to stop me talking about it,' he said a trifle grimly, and Mary thought that whatever he might say, it *was* important to him that the Queen should acknowledge him and see that at last, his exploits received a measure of renown.

The time passed all too quickly for Mary, and it seemed only a little while before John Brewer was rowing back to the ship, to tell Drake that he thought everything would be all right.

'The Queen says you have done well,' he announced triumphantly. 'And she will take care of you and your crew, and stop any possible trouble the Spaniards may wish to make. She wants you to go to

London as soon as possible, and take with you certain curiosities from your voyage around the world, so that she may see such wonders for herself.'

Drake laughed exuberantly. 'She shall see curiosities that will make her eyes start from her head,' he said. 'And the rest is to be lodged in Saltash Castle, eh? And Edmund Tremayne is to keep it safe until my return? Fair enough, we will take the *Golden Hind* across the Tamar and off-load the holds there, where the risk of infection is small. Then we shall go to London and the Queen shall hear my story.'

'She may not want to hear the story, her main interest will probably lie in what she sees,' Mary said with a laugh, but Drake shook his head. 'No, she'll want to hear the story,' he assured his wife. 'After all, she wanted Philip annoyed; she is human enough to resent the way he is trying to force her hand, the way he maltreats her subjects and assists in every effort against our country, even paying people to attempt to assassinate her and her advisers. She will delight in the tale of our voyage.'

'What shall I do, Frank?' asked Mary, rather wistfully. 'Shall I go back to the Plymouth house? It will seem lonely without you.'

'Why, of course you must not be lonely,' Drake said quickly. 'You've been without me for three years! You shall come to London and we'll lodge together, and Johnny shall accompany us. Would you like that, cousin?'

Johnny's blue eyes lit up. 'I would prefer it to anything you could name,' he replied with prompt simplicity. 'When shall we leave?'

'First we must sail the ship round to the castle,' Drake said. 'A day—maybe two or three—to off-load, and then another day to pack the horses. I shall arrange for a skeleton crew to sail the *Golden Hind* round to Deptford, which is free from the plague, and near enough to London for me to keep an eye on her. Yes, we can be on the road to London, all being well, in five days from now.'

So Mary sailed with the *Golden Hind* across Cattewater, into the Hamoaze and finally across the mouth of the Tamar and up to the watergate of Saltash Castle. Here she saw the treasure for the first time—the only woman whose eyes would rest on it before the great Queen Elizabeth herself had seen and marvelled. Mary handled the beautiful materials with tears in her eyes, for Frank had chosen the loveliest of everything for her, and she was given china so fragile that she could see the light through it when she held it up to the sky, and materials rich and glossy, fine as cobweb, warm and light.

'When we get to London you'll buy nothing but the best,' Drake promised her, smiling. 'We will go to the Royal Exchange and anything you want you shall have.'

So the little company of three set off on horseback, riding beside the packponies with their heavy burdens. A picked bunch of men from the *Golden Hind* rode with them, for Drake had no intention of being robbed of his hard won riches, and his men were in complete agreement with that sentiment!

They found lodgings easily enough but Drake could not stay to help them settle in for he wanted his goods to be taken straight to the Queen, so whilst he and Johnny continued their journey Mary and Becky hired servants, shopped for the essentials they needed, and prepared the bedchambers.

Katherine Hawkins, warned of their arrival by her husband, arrived to find Mary and Becky enveloped in aprons and mob caps to keep themselves as clean as possible whilst they dusted and polished, moving furniture and hanging tapestries.

'Are you going to get fresh rushes? These are stale,' said Katherine, stirring the grey and dusty hay on the floor with a disdainful toe. 'If you would like me to do so, I will get one of my wenches to go down to Gracechurch Street and bring in some bundles of clean stuff and then I can strew the floors for you.'

'Phew, the dust we're raising tells me that we'd best not spread fresh rushes and herbs until the floors have had a thorough scrubbing,' Mary said, pushing her hair back from her forehead and leaving a dirty mark across the bridge of her nose. 'But thank you, Katherine. Could you ask one of your maids to order me rushes for a couple of days time? By then the place should be sweet and wholesome once more.'

'All right. And why don't you and Frank come round to our house for a meal tonight, when Frank returns from seeing the Queen,' urged Katherine. 'It will save you the bother of preparing a meal when you are so busy with cleaning and settling in.'

'It's kind of you, Katherine, but I don't think I can accept. Frank will have had a long and tiring day by the time he arrives home, and we don't yet know whether the story is going to have a happy ending, though the Queen has been kind. But there are others—many others—who are eager to bow to the wishes of the Spanish ambassador. So I think we will eat plainly and quietly at home, tonight.'

'You're probably wise,' Katherine admitted. 'I know John would hate to find himself having to be entertained by a friend, no matter how close, when he is tired. But I will call round again in a day or so, to see how you're getting along.'

So Katherine left her, and Mary resigned herself once more to wait for Francis Drake.

13

LADY MARY

'Well, Becky! The Queen knighted my husband and now he is Sir Francis—and of course, I am Lady Mary. I was presented to the Queen, Becky, though I was so shy I scarcely dared raise my eyes to her face. But I was glad I wore my new gown of yellow silk for all eyes were upon it, and no one really noticed me!'

'I wish I could have seen you, curtseying to the Queen,' Becky said wistfully. 'And I'm bound everyone noticed your pretty face, for all your yellow gown is so beautiful.'

'One person noticed me,' Mary agreed with a chuckle. 'Do you remember Master

Jan Carew? He asked to be remembered to you!'

'Never say he came slap up to speak to you, milady? The bold rascal, with all that there is between you,' said Becky, shocked.

'All that there *was* between us,' corrected Mary. 'And that is best forgotten, or at least not spoken about. Jan is restless now, with his time as a soldier finished for a while he wanted to ask Frank whether another voyage was in prospect. So he will be coming to the house to talk to my husband, Becky, and we shall be good friends once more.'

'I think, upon reflection, that he was wise to approach you,' Becky said. 'After all, he is a Plymouth man and when we return to Devon as no doubt we shall do shortly, your paths are bound to cross. Now that he has spoken to you as a friend, there need be no further awkwardness.'

But rather to Mary's dismay, she discovered that Drake had no intention of returning to Plymouth for a while.

'There is a plan afoot to assist Don Antonio of Portugal to regain his kingdom,' Drake told his wife. 'I and a number of other important men—Leicester, Walsingham, Sussex—will be examining the proposed methods of aiding Portugal whilst with any luck we also annoy Spain, and perhaps capture ourselves more of her ill-gotten gains from the Indies.'

So Mary had, perforce, to stay in London. She lay in bed one night a few weeks later, telling herself firmly that she would gladly renounce Plymouth in order to be near Frank, whilst staring into the darkness above her head, trying not to pine for the sea air which would be blowing now over their Plymouth home.

'You could be happy enough, Mary, if you chose.' Drake spoke abruptly out of the velvet dark, making Mary jump. She had thought him asleep after a strenuous day and lying between the sheets, feeling sorry for herself, it almost seemed as though he had read her thoughts.

'You can't make a silk purse out of a sow's ear,' she said resentfully, aloud. 'You want to make a grand lady out of me, don't you? Well, you can't. If you wanted a noble lady for a wife, you should have married one.'

His silence was like an accusation and Mary shrugged off the covers and sat up, pulling back the bedhanging so that the starlight lit the room faintly. 'I have tried, Frank,' she said pleadingly. 'But I'm all *wrong*. My voice is too quiet, yet every word I utter speaks of the Devonshire country. If I dance too much I cough, and that annoys you; if I don't dance you say I'm being unsociable. So now I find it better not to mix with our noble friends except when they come to the house. And you should admit that things have been better since I allowed you to take up the social round without me.'

Drake said crossly, 'All you need is a bit of courage, woman! Do you think that I find it easy mixing with men who've known the court since childhood? Half of them dislike me very heartily, I assure you.'

'But you have self-confidence, because you've proved your worth,' said Mary desperately. 'I put on the beautiful clothes you buy me, and look like a milkmaid who has stolen into her mistress's chamber to try on her finery!'

'That's because you won't let me hire a proper lady's maid to do your hair and show you how to wear court dresses,' Drake said sullenly. '"Becky is good enough for me",' he mimicked savagely.

Mary felt the colour burn in her cheeks. 'A lady's maid would despise me,' she said, with a catch in her voice. 'She might teach me how to wear clothes properly and do my hair for me but she couldn't make me believe that I looked like a noble lady. Oh Frank, do stop trying to make me into something I am not!'

'But Mary, if *I* can do it ...'

'Yes, you can do it. And do you know why, Frank? Because you don't *care* that half the court snigger behind their hands, say that you're conceited and boastful, that you buy your way to favour. They laugh because Burghley won't accept your gold, they call you the pirate of the unknown world, and the Queen's corsair. You have no shame, Frank! Or rather, your self-esteem and conceit are so great that you don't believe anyone is better than you are.'

Shaken by her own courage in giving vent to the thoughts she had harboured for some weeks, Mary lay back, wondering what Frank would say. To her relief, however, he gave a laugh of genuine amusement.

'Why, Mary, of course I believe I'm as good as the next man!' he said honestly. 'I've done something that a lot of people think is wonderful, but let them wait, that's all. I shall do things that they think more wonderful yet, and in their hearts I believe they know it. Who would ever have guessed that I should be knighted before John Hawkins, for instance? That I should have Frobisher's hatred for my popularity, who never deigned to acknowledge my existence before? But I've tried to carry you with me, little one. I've opened doors for us both, and have had to walk through them alone. Believe me, I've had a hard job sometimes, not to run away from the very court ladies who snigger at me behind their hands, but I've set my teeth and told myself that I've more guts and brains in my little finger than their husbands and lovers have in the whole of their long, elegant bodies. I'm short, and sturdily built, and many make fun of my low stature, which they say only exceeds my low station. Why the hell should I let such small-minded people humiliate me? I stick out my chin and make a fantastic claim and no one dares to gainsay me because in their hearts they believe me to be capable of fulfilling my boasts.'

'We're so different, Frank,' Mary said apologetically. 'You see, you've have adventures and mixed with the gentlemen who accompanied you on the voyage, and you've known Spanish noblemen and English ones, too. But for me, one day it was a little house in Plymouth with money running short and no knowledge as to whether I was a widow or not, and the next I was catapulted into the cream of society as Lady Mary Drake and expected to live up to my new station. I am most truly sorry.'

Drake rolled over in bed and pulled her into his arms. 'My love, you've done your best, and I know it. I'm sorry too; sorry that I've brought you up here and made you unhappy. But soon you'll be happy again, and healthier too, I hope, for London doesn't suit you. That nasty cough will disappear when we are back in the clean fresh air of the Devonshire countryside.'

'Oh, are we going back to Plymouth

soon then?' Mary asked eagerly. 'I shall be happier there, and more able to help you with your social life, for I've known the people so long that I am not shy or ill at ease with them.'

'It may not be very soon,' Drake said cautiously, 'but you know the Grenvilles, my love? And their home near Plymouth, Buckland Abbey?'

'I saw Sir Richard a few times when he was Sheriff of the County; he's a handsome man, isn't he? Katherine is friendly with his wife, Lady Mary Grenville, and told me she is a charming woman. Why, Frank?'

'I've bought Buckland,' said Drake nonchalantly. 'Sir Richard has made many improvements, turning it from an abbey into the pleasant dwelling house that it now is, and the grounds are very fine. I have kept on those servants who did not wish to go with Sir Richard, and you will have Becky for your own personal maid, of course. What do you think of that?'

'Oh, Frank!' gasped Mary, putting her

arms round his neck. 'A home in the country! And Buckland Abbey! When my mother hears of it, she'll be almost proud of me!'

'Yes, my darling. But how do you feel, yourself? Are you pleased that you will live in such a place?'

'To live in such a house is the height of my dreams,' said Mary. 'Why, Frank, I couldn't be happier.'

And for the first time for many weeks Mary fell asleep without many wakeful hours of tossing and turning, and slumbered soundly all night long, dreaming of the delights she would soon know.

They travelled down to Plymouth slowly, riding beside the coaches laden with hangings, tapestries and pieces of furniture which they had brought to beautify their new home. The journey had a startling resemblance to a Royal Progress, Mary was surprised to see, and as they passed through the dreaming countryside of early summer, every one wanted to meet them, to entertain them. And Mary, drinking in the sweet fresh air of the meadows and lanes, was content that they should travel slowly.

'We will go first to Buckland to settle into the new house, and then we must move back to our house in Looe Street for a while, so that I can busy myself with affairs of Plymouth and see to the building and provision of ships for the next enterprise,' Drake said, not content ever to be merely travelling, with no particular purpose in view. Mary smiled and acquiesced.

When they arrived at Buckland, Drake, who had been a guest there during the Grenvilles' time, sat on his horse and watched Mary's face with genuine pleasure in her delight.

'Frank, it is the most perfect place,' she said, 'But how the Grenvilles must have hated parting with it! I wonder why Sir Richard sold it to you?'

Drake's forehead wrinkled into a frown. 'He didn't exactly sell it to *me*, since it was done through others, but I'm fairly sure he knew I was to be the eventual purchaser,' he said. 'He had wanted to undertake my voyage through the Straits of Magellan, you know, and would have done so, had the Queen not held him back. He has never grudged me one iota of my success, never snubbed me or behaved in an insolent fashion towards me, as many men have done who think themselves better than he. But I believe he feels that he could never be the first man of Plymouth again, and as such, he preferred to sell this magnificent manor and take up his residence on one of his other estates.'

Mary nodded. 'Yes, I do see. It's understandable. But oh, Frank, what a house! And the grounds! See—a bowling green where you and your friends may play at bowls, a rose garden, a knot garden, herbs and fruit. There is nothing missing, it is like a dream come true, my darling.'

And for Mary, Buckland was a dream come true. Frank, for all his talk and plans, did not seem about to leave her again after all; the expedition would be led by others though he would have his hand in the planning of it. And even when they moved back to Looe Street, with people constantly in and out of the house, Mary found it easy to be Lady Mary of Plymouth. Entertaining at Buckland was a joy, because the house was only partly furnished and so she and Frank agreed that only their most intimate friends should visit it, until their furnishing was complete. Mary quite understood that for the moment at any rate, the house in Plymouth was more suitable for her husband's work, but she enjoyed Plymouth the more for knowing that Buckland awaited them, whenever they had a few days to spare in quietness.

She soon took it for granted that Drake's plans necessitated sudden trips to London, Tavistock or Exeter, and when he left her hurriedly, she did not attempt to accompany him, for 'I ride fast when I am upon the Queen's business,' he would tell her with a smile. But though she did not understand his work, she was pleased to help him to entertain friends and business acquaintances when the need arose.

Becky, seeing her mistress being a gracious if somewhat reserved hostess to her husband's many guests, said approvingly, 'What did I tell you, Lady Mary? You've soon settled to it! Yet despite the weather growing clement, you have not yet lost your cough. I'll tell young Job from the stables to ride over to Buckland and bring back some honey from the hives. Heather honey is good for coughs, I've heard tell.'

Mary nodded carelessly. In fact, she was rather concerned about the cough, which gave her little rest when she had been riding or enjoying vigorous exercise. She knew it could be nothing much, for the roses bloomed in her cheeks and her friends congratulated her on her good health, but she had hoped that the summer would bring easement. Yet here it was, August, and still the cough racked her. She shrugged away the niggling worry about her own health and concentrated on her husband's career. For Katherine Hawkins, very much her friend, had told her that she believed the people of Plymouth were talking of electing Drake as their Mayor, when election time came in the Autumn.

'It would be good to be Mayor,' Drake said rather gloomily. 'After all these months of trying to bring together a force of English and French to secure the bastard, Don Antonio, upon the throne of Portugal, he has brought about a failure by his own greed, before the fleet had even been decided upon. I will forget the sea, and great affairs, for a while, and become a landsman.'

'What did Don Antonio do?' Mary asked curiously. 'I thought the captains quarrelled, and Bingham exceeded his authority, and you believed Fenton had Catholic sympathies, or something of that sort. Nothing really to do with Don Antonio himself.'

Drake chuckled unwillingly. 'Something of that sort,' he conceded. 'To tell you the truth, my love, it seems that Walsingham was more indispensable than I had thought. As you know, he is now our Ambassador in Paris, and from the moment that he left to take up his duties there, and Leicester took over, things began to go wrong. Walsingham is not only a leader of men, he is a strategist and has a great deal of foresight and common sense. Leicester, alas, is not a man whom other men reward with their immediate trust and affection. And anyway, with the best will in the world and the co-operation of every man involved in the enterprise, he could not have done anything with Don Antonio in his present mood, and the Queen in hers. Don Antonio boasts of the diamond which we hold as his surety—God, that diamond is not worth a twentieth part of that which has been spent by us in England upon an empty venture! For Don Antonio demands more men, more ships, more cannon, and the Queen knows none of us can afford to pay out continually, in return for grumbles and more demands. So now she says no more, go with what you have or do not go at all. And Don Antonio sulks and the captains, as you say, quarrel. But let us talk of pleasanter things.'

So for a while, it seemed that Drake rested, though he spent long hours with John Hawkins, planning to build up the Queen's navy so that she had a decent array of fighting ships to turn to when she was in need, instead of always having to borrow from the private owners.

And when October came, Sir Francis was elected as Mayor of Plymouth, and Mary was his Mayoress. It was the proudest day of her life.

14

MAYOR OF PLYMOUTH

Mary sat in her garden, feeling the sun on her shoulders through the silk of her gown as she stitched quickly and neatly at yet another row of embroidery round the neck of her new shift. Since Drake had become Mayor she had grown at ease as the civic hostess at the many banquets given by the town in honour of distinguished visitors. But she found that new clothes were an enjoyable necessity, and frequently trimmed and embroidered her shifts herself, in the colour which blended best with a new gown or partlet.

The heat of the sun was pleasant, but the beads of sweat formed on Mary's fingers making the needle feel slippery and somehow heavy. The cough, which Drake had thought merely the result of over-tension and the grimy air of London had not left her, and sometimes a strange heaviness, a lassitude, came over her, making her every movement an effort. But she hid this affliction from her husband, knowing how it worried him to hear her cough, and how much more he would have worried if he had known of the effort it gave her on occasion, to drag her heavy limbs upstairs.

She rested her work in her lap for a moment, and thought about her health. Was she a sick woman? She had spat blood recently when the cough had racked her, but then she'd spat blood when she was a young girl and no harm had come of it. Shrugging, she dismissed her health as unimportant. It was probably something trivial that would pass, given time.

Drake was out on this bright afternoon inspecting the fortifications on the hoe, and on the island of St Nicholas. Once, she thought with a wry smile, he had been a frightened child hiding on that island from those who would have persecuted him for his parents' religious beliefs. But had he ever thought, then, that one day he would walk majestically round that same island, ensuring that the aldermen of Plymouth had the work of its defences in hand?

A step from the house made her turn, and there stood Frank, smiling fondly at the pretty picture of his wife in a gown of blush-pink silk, bent over her work.

'My love, I've told Becky to pack me a bag. I'm off to London.'

'London, Frank? But why? There's plenty of work for you here! Already you've studied and improved the defences of the town, improved conditions for the ships which come into Sutton Pool, and have tried to make the lot of the women of the waterfront easier, so that they do not have to sink to immorality. Can your work in London be more important than these things?'

Drake sighed and pulled his ear. 'I really ought to go, Mary. And in person this time, rather than send a representative.'

'But why in the heat of summer? Already plague precautions are under way in Plymouth: temporary housing is being erected on the hoe and there will be tents at Cattedown shortly. Why, you know yourself that the aldermen have paid a Scavenger to keep the streets as clean as possible.'

'I'll probably not be in London long. There is a further plan afoot, you see, to send another expedition to the Indies. I shall stay in London only long enough to discuss the plans with the Queen, Leicester, and one or two others.'

So he left her, his mood optimistic and cheerful as always, and Mary moved herself and her servant out to Buckland so that in his absence they might work on the empty house.

But the pleasures of the countryside were shortlived. After they had settled in, Mary sat with the bailiff one morning seeing the accounts when a messenger from London arrived to speak to her.

As soon as the man had delivered his message, Mary sent for her personal maid. 'Becky,' she said. 'There has been an attempt on my husband's life. Thomas Doughty, the man Sir Francis condemned for treason whilst on the voyage of circumnavigation, has a brother, young John Doughty. The wild young fool has tried to avenge his brother's death by trying to kill Frank. I don't yet understand the ins and outs of the business but I soon shall, since my husband wants us to join him in London.'

They reached the city in only two days, to find that the attempted assassination was as complicated as Mary had feared. It appeared that the attempt had not been Doughty's own plan and that Spain had been behind him in the shape of an agitator named Mason who was embroiled in the plot.

'Do you walk the streets in fear of your life, Frank?' Mary asked anxiously, and was reassured by his answer.

'Indeed no, my darling! The King of Spain wants me dead, but who does he have to choose as his executioner? A foolish, hot-headed young man who feels himself wronged, who has already laid a year in prison for a crime against the late Earl of Essex. And Doughty, as you know, bungled his attempt. I cannot believe that someone with no personal hatred for me, such as Doughty had to spur him on, would be able to carry it out. But I fear Doughty has as good as signed his death warrant. They will not let him go free to harbour malice against any man who crosses him.'

'How did they find out that Doughty wasn't just trying to lay the blame on Mason?' asked Mary.

'They put Mason to the torture, and he told them names, gave them all the information they wanted. It was a genuine attempt on Doughty's part which he might have made in any case. I don't believe, myself, that he would have taken money for having his revenge.'

'Torture! Did they have to use such means?' Mary said slowly.

'I believe so. Mason was a good agent, and would not have spoken otherwise.'

'What will happen now, Frank? Will there be a trial?'

'I think not. They will be imprisoned, and perhaps Mason will be exiled. But a trial would raise too much speculation and there might be repercussions.'

Mary walked over to the window of the lodgings Frank had hired, and looked out onto the garden, which sloped down to the Thames. The house was large and pleasant, and Mary remembered how often she and Frank had envied those in a financial position to be able to afford such a dwelling. But now she wondered about the much vaunted advantages of dwelling on Thames-side. The river here was noisy with the sound of the forciers continually splashing as they churned water out of the Thames, and boats were as thick as lilies on the water with the cries of the oarsmen and the noise of their passengers sounding clearly across the water.

'What are you thinking of, love?'

Mary turned from the window and smiled at her husband. 'I was thinking how we have risen in the world, to have a house with a garden running down to the river, and I was wondering why you've taken such a large house, if you intended to return to Plymouth soon.'

'Ah, yes. Well, sweetheart, there are some matters concerning this new expedition to the Indies which need my attention. The Earl of Leicester is doing his utmost to aid the enterprise but unfortunately he and I cannot agree on the appointment of Edward Fenton as Admiral of the fleet. He is a quarrelsome and conceited fellow, but Leicester cannot see his faults.'

'Then why waste your breath if your

words can alter nothing?'

'Well for one thing, our Johnny sails with the fleet, although I cannot. He is in command of the *Francis,* a small ship but handily built and speedy. Your friend Carew sails with Johnny which will be good for both, since they have become firm friends. There were efforts to get Johnny excluded from a command, probably because Fenton realised that I'd work against his own position, so he is taking revenge on my young relative. But Johnny is a good sailor and will make a first-rate captain. I'll not see his future ruined by Fenton's spite.'

'Well, if it's for Johnny's sake that we stay in London I'll make the best of it,' said Mary lightly, though her heart thumped at the mention of Jan Carew. 'Tell me, Frank, is the voyage truly a trade effort? Has no one mentioned silver or gold?'

Drake grinned. 'The purpose of the voyage—the avowed purpose at any rate—is to open up regular trade with the Moluccas. But I imagine few of the mariners who are interested will banish dreams of another *Cacafuego* from their minds.'

'I thought it was too good to be true,' remarked Mary. 'When does the enterprise sail, then? Do any of our other friends sail as well?'

'William Hawkins goes, and the date of sailing depends as usual, on the weather. They don't want to voyage through the Straits of Magellan because folk say it bears the taint of piracy but they will take the longer route by the open sea around the islands which lie to the side of the straits. And in the meantime, I must work to make sure that all goes as well as possible for the venture.'

They stayed in London for several weeks of that summer, then came the summons to return to Devonshire, and with the speed which characterised all his movements, Drake organised their journey back at once.

'We cannot return to Buckland yet,' he said to Mary's timid request, 'For the enterprise *is* to be led by Fenton—the Muscovy Company have shares in the venture and he is their choice—so I want to be in Plymouth to ensure that all set out in amity, at least.'

Mary could see that the business preyed on his nerves, that he was plagued by the dreadful certainty that only he himself could ensure the success of the mission.

'But the Queen wants me in England for a while, yet,' he told his wife gloomily, and when Mary said, 'Then that makes two of us,' he scarcely smiled.

The waiting time which was so filled with worries for Frank, however, was a happy time for Mary. She enjoyed having the young company of Johnny Drake and William Hawkins about the house, with the swaggering young men who were their friends. And though seeing Jan Carew could only be a bitter-sweet experience, Mary could still enjoy his company.

The trouble that Drake feared soon became apparent, for though men were willing and eager to serve under young Drake or young Hawkins, few of them wished to sail under Fenton, whom they neither liked nor trusted. Fenton naturally enough resented this so it was with no real surprise that Drake discovered that with the fleet ready to sail, Fenton had stolen away in his ship like a thief in the night, leaving Johnny and William and their crews behind.

Frank, however, knew both lads to be fine seamen and undertook to round up their men for them whilst they prepared their vessels for sea.

So Mary stood once more on the Hoe, waving to the ship which carried not only her nephew but her lover also, into the silvery distance, rich with promise.

'Don't worry, my love, they'll catch up with Fenton,' said Drake scornfully as he saw the tears standing in Mary's eyes. 'Why, young Hawkins is second in command of the venture! How dare he treat a good man in such a fashion! If I were John Hawkins I'd see him in serious trouble for this.'

Mary was glad that Frank thought her tears merely of worry that the craft might be left behind. And why indeed should she weep to see Jan leave her, when he was happy to do so and when in any event, they could never mean anything to each other, now, except in friendship? But she dragged her thoughts from Jan, to remind Frank that it was not easy for John Hawkins to quarrel with Edward Fenton. 'For Fenton's wife, Thomasine, and John's own dear Katherine are sisters. It is bad enough when a quarrel flares in a fleet of ships, but when it flares within a family it can soon become a feud.'

'I suppose you're right,' Frank admitted. 'Well, let us take ourselves off to Buckland for a few months, Mary! I've work to do in Plymouth of course—the fortifications of the town are being strengthened, and a shelter is to be built on the hoe with a mariner's compass set up. Then there is a banquet which we must attend for Sir Richard Grenville, who will be visiting the town. He wishes to talk over a plan for colonising some remote part of the globe.'

'Would you rather not return to Buckland?' Mary asked, laughing.

'Well, we shall have to be in Plymouth for the election of the new Mayor in the autumn,' Drake said sheepishly. 'Shall we spend Christmas at Buckland, then?'

'That would be lovely. Now let us tell the Hawkins that their son is aboard his ship and running before a stiff breeze, to rejoin his fleet.'

Together, they walked slowly back into the town, and Mary spared not another glance at the two small ships heading so steadily towards the silver line of the horizon. But her thoughts went with them as they sailed out into the unknown world.

15

THE NEW YEAR

'What a wonderful Christmas we've had; one of the best I can remember,' Mary said contentedly. 'I've so enjoyed having Annie and her children in the house, I shall miss them so much. But at least they stayed as long as they could, and I'm sure they enjoyed themselves as much as we did.'

'Yes indeed. A real family Christmas,' Frank said, but though his words were cheerful, his tone was anxious. Mary had worked too hard for her health's sake, he knew, when the plague had struck hot at Plymouth people during the late summer and early autumn so that Christmastide with its extra cooking and entertaining had fallen upon a woman already worn out.

He looked anxiously at her now, in the flickering firelight. She was so *thin!* The hands she held out to the blazing logs were like fine porcelain and through the skin, turned rosy by the firelight, he could see her bones looking pitifully small and frail. The cough had not gone, as they had hoped it would. Instead, she had grown more careful to hide the signs of it. And he had noticed that when the children romped and played Mary had joined in at first, only to sink into a chair under the pretext of fastening a lace or a buckle.

Mary saw his anxiety, and smiled peacefully. She was too contented to try to reassure him and indeed, sitting safe and warm in front of the roaring fire, she found it difficult to believe that she *was* ill. Death was something that sought other people out, coming in a variety of grim disguises. Surely it could not happen to a young woman, smiled on by fortune, who had spent many weary years living frugally, waiting for her man?

She tried to shake off the fear that gripped her when she thought of death. She had accomplished so little in her life! No children, no mark of importance to set upon the page which her husband had already made rich with his exploits. If I die now, how will they know me, those that come after, she thought frantically. Will I just be a name, soon forgotten? Mary Newman, the farmer's daughter, who married herself the best man who ever came out of Devon?

She felt a sob fighting for release rise in her heart. It seemed cruelly hard that she should be just a cold name on a cold gravestone when she was twenty-eight, and had her life before her.

Frank saw the subtle change come over her expression and reached out his hand to grasp hers. 'Are you unhappy, my darling?' he said softly. 'Do you feel unwell?'

With the touch of his warm, confident hand on hers, the moment of fear died away as though it had never been. After the shortest of pauses she was able to reply steadily, 'Why, I am very happy, Frank. And I feel well enough; just a little tired perhaps. But very happy.' And what was more, she meant it. For happiness is of the moment, she told herself. Even if I die tomorrow, I shall have known this happiness. And why should I worry what mark I leave on life? Frank had made the name of Drake so renowned that any who bore it would be honoured.

She sighed contentedly and took an apple from the dish. Biting into it, feeling the crisp flesh yield before her healthy teeth, it was impossible to seriously consider dying.

★ ★ ★ ★

'Mary, my dear, I've some bad news I'm afraid. You'd better sit down.'

Drake came into the room in his riding dress, aglow from the cold bite of sleet but without his usual cheery smile.

Mary had been toasting her hands in front of the fire, but at his words she moved back from it a little, sinking obediently into the nearest chair.

'Whatever is it, Frank? It's not like you to frighten me. Has something gone amiss with your plans to water the ships from a conduit, instead of pumping from the wells?'

'Oh Mary, if it were only that! It is the venture to the Indies. Our Johnny decided Fenton was mismanaging the expedition, and sailed off with the *Francis*, determined to pass through the straits by himself if need be. But his ship was wrecked in the river Plate, and ...'

'He's dead? Our Johnny was killed? Drowned?'

'It is not as bad as that, thank God. Or perhaps—but no, he is not dead, but a captive of the Spaniards.'

'You were going to say he might have been better dead,' Mary said, her eyes filled with horror. 'To think of our bright, golden-haired lad being in the hands of those evil men.'

But her mind held another terror; that Jan might be dead, and she would never know. He could have been her husband, and safe at home tilling his fields and fathering children upon her; but instead, had he felt his life flickering out as his head sank beneath the vast and uncaring waters of the river Plate? Or did he lie in some dark, noisome dungeon, cursing the fate that had led him there, and the woman who had given him her body once, and then denied him marriage? She moaned softly, and Frank took her hands.

'Mary, don't despair. Johnny is young, and has great charm. Furthermore, he speaks Spanish fluently. He may well charm them into allowing us to ransom him.'

'Not once they know he is related to you,' Mary said dully. 'They wanted your life badly enough to try assassination—do you think they will give Johnny up?'

And Frank was silent, for he thought the same himself.

Presently Mary rallied a little. 'What of William Hawkins? Did he not accompany Johnny?' she asked.

'No. He could not, for Fenton had removed him from his command and brought him home in irons. The Hawkins family will not be pleased, and they have always been hot against Spain and have considerable influence with people who matter. Through him we might win Johnny's freedom.'

Mary had to pretend to agree for Frank's peace of mind, but in her heart she was sure appeals would be useless. Whenever she thought of Jan now, she felt as though she had been given a mortal blow, and living itself seemed less important. Whether a prisoner or dead, she felt responsible for his fate and her hold on life began, imperceptibly, to loosen.

For a couple of nights she fought against nightmares where he died as John

Oxenham had done, swinging high on a gallows against a tropic sky, or rotted in a Spanish prison until madness or death claimed him.

Worn out by lack of sleep she went into the kitchen to talk to Becky, who stood, red-faced and cheerful, turning meat on the spit.

'You know Master Carew was on board the *Francis*, Becky?' she said as the maid left the task to the kitchen wench and began to walk through the big kitchens which were still unfurnished and unused. 'Well, I do not know whether he is dead or a prisoner, and I feel that to die without knowing if he lives and suffers, or has gone before me, is unbearable.'

'Why, Lady Mary, you shouldn't talk like that,' Becky said, shocked. 'You aren't going to die tomorrow! Why should you think you will die before the news comes back from Spain regarding the prisoners?'

Mary shrugged impatiently. 'I'm sorry I put it in that way, then, Becky. But you

313

see, I blame myself for Master Carew's fate, whatever it may be. If I had married him, as he wished, he would never have taken ship with Johnny. He was content with his fields and farm, and would have been more content with me beside him.'

'Your duty was to the master,' Becky said sternly. 'You cannot be blamed for Master Jan falling in love with you, for you gave him no encouragement. Now just you stop blaming yourself, for no one else does I'll be bound.'

Mary turned away to walk back to the living quarters, when a cough caught at her. Twisting round she grabbed a strip of linen from Becky's hands and buried her face in it, trying to stifle the noise.

'I'll get vinegar and water to sponge your brow,' Becky began, when a dreadful rasping cough broke from Mary's lips seeming as though it would tear the heart from her chest, and a great gush of blood followed it.

Mary fell forward over the stone sink,

Becky screamed, and Drake, who had been searching for his wife, ran into the room. His face turned white as his shirt at the sight of Mary's head dangling over the crimson-washed stone and he crossed the room in a couple of strides and lifted her up in his arms.

'Get a warming pan into her bed, Becky,' he ordered tersely, 'and send one of the grooms for the doctor. Hurry!'

He carried his wife carefully up the stairs marvelling at her frail weight in his arms, for she seemed no heavier than a child. In the bedchamber, Becky was warming the sheets whilst another maid knelt on the hearth, kindling the fire that had been laid ready for the evening.

When Mary regained consciousness it seemed the most natural thing in the world that she should be lying here, in her own bed, where she had lain so many times before. What was unnatural was the heaviness of her limbs which felt like lumps of lead so that even to turn her head a little on the pillow was an enormous effort.

Frank sat close by the bed and she smiled at him; a small, faint smile which showed more than anything how tired she was. He spoke to her in a quiet, sad voice, and she smiled again but was afraid to answer for fear it might make her cough and when her silence made him weep, she could find no words to comfort him.

The doctor came and looked grave, though he spoke hearteningly to Drake and left a recipe for something to ease Mary's cough should it be possible to administer it to her. But Mary met his wise old eyes, and read the message there more clearly than her husband could. Strangely, it no longer troubled her, for she smiled again.

Drake waited throughout the night close by her bed, in the hope that she might speak to him, but she lay motionless, sometimes with her eyes closed, sometimes gazing at his face. In the early hours of the morning it seemed that she wanted to be raised in the bed and Drake hurried to lift her, hoping that she might now take some nourishment. But the movement made her draw in her breath sharply, and the cough she had fought to contain broke forth and with it, a river of blood which soaked into the bedclothes yet still reached out its flood to turn more white to crimson.

'Becky!' called Drake, with deep anguish, and the maid came through from the closet where she had been lying, fully-clothed and ready.

They lay Mary back on her pillows and Drake chafed her slender hands whilst Becky mopped the blood from her skin, but suddenly something in the pale calm face of his wife made him grope for the polished steel mirror and hold it to her lips.

No tell-tale mist blurred the surface, and Drake moved her hands so that they were crossed on her breast and closed her eyelids over her peaceful blue eyes.

'Will you make the necessary arrangement, Becky?' Drake said stiffly through quivering lips. 'I must tell her sisters.'

When they left the room, the silence of the winter's dawn settled in the air, with the first faint cold grey of morning creeping into the night sky and no bird yet stirring.

The fire settled in the grate, the candle burned lower, and if a sound haunted that place, it was of Mary's own unspoken fear.

'She married Francis Drake and was buried in her twenty-ninth year. We know nothing more of her.'

The publishers hope that this book has given you enjoyable reading. Large Print Books are especially designed to be as easy to see and hold as possible. If you wish a complete list of our books, please ask at your local library or write directly to: Dales Large Print Books, Long Preston, North Yorkshire, BD23 4ND, England.

This Large Print Book for the Partially sighted, who cannot read normal print, is published under the auspices of

THE ULVERSCROFT FOUNDATION